ANNIE TRIES NOT TO

and

ANNIE'S CASE BOOK

JOY REID

Cover Page Illustrated by Sue Millar-Smith

Order this book online at www.trafford.com
or email orders@trafford.com

Most Trafford titles are also available at major online book retailers.

Printed in the United States of America.

ISBN: 978-1-4269-4751-3 (sc)
ISBN: 978-1-4269-4752-0 (hc)
ISBN: 978-1-4269-4753-7 (e)

Library of Congress Control Number: 2010916841

Trafford rev. 12/27/2010

 www.trafford.com

North America & International
toll-free: 1 888 232 4444 (USA & Canada)
phone: 250 383 6864 ♦ fax: 812 355 4082

To all my family with love

ANNIE TRIES NOT TO

Joy Reid

CHAPTER 1

"THEY'VE A BIT OF a problem at the college", said Maggie Hurst, Head of the George Pound School, to her friend Annie Butcher, a widow and Head of Biology and temporarily acting as Deputy Head.

"I don't want to know," said Annie dismissively. She had looked up from her marking as Maggie entered the staff room but she returned to her papers in a determined way. Maggie ignored what she considered to be a negative attitude.

"Lance thought you'd be interested," she continued.

"Well, I'm not." Annie knew that Maggie was referring to events last year when they had all been involved in a case that had included murder, illegal immigrants and an extra girl in school.

"Lance suggested I talk to you, it's worrying him and he does like peace and quiet," Maggie was almost pleading, "he doesn't get much at home."

Annie was aware that Maggie's husband liked to put his problems on other shoulders, in their former troubles he had known far more than he would admit to knowing. He was head of music at the local teacher training college, he did not like outside interruptions.

"Whatever it is, it's nothing to do with me," Annie was equally resolved not to be involved.

"You were right in the middle of things before," Maggie went on.

"I didn't want to be, it happened to me, I didn't instigate it."

Maggie had no intention of giving up, she had sheltered Lance for many years, and was not going to give up on something that was troubling him now.

"We thought that with the police in your pocket . . ."

"What do you mean?" Annie interrupted, "just one small non-affair with a detective inspector does not mean that I have the whole force at my beck and call!" She was indignant.

"Have it your own way," replied Maggie for when Annie had raised her voice other members of staff raised their heads and were beginning to take notice. Maggie moved nearer to Annie and spoke softly, "It's a missing student and it's puzzling Lance, he doesn't like to be involved."

"Amen to that," retorted Annie, "and, as if you didn't know, I have a class waiting," she prepared to depart, "as if we didn't have enough troubles of our own."

Maggie decided on different tactics, "Why don't you come to supper tonight?" she asked.

Annie was at the door about to leave but she turned back and with a more cheerful smile and said, "I'd love to."

They did have troubles at the school but these were of a wider nature, not like the temporary gloom of the day when, in the middle of the summer term with everyone's ideas fixed on being outside, it was pouring with rain. Sport was out of the question when watery pools dotted the playing fields and macs and dripping students drifted about the school. Annie felt justified in dismissing Lance's troubles, she was busy and did not want other people's worries.

Events of the year before had brought a certain notoriety to the school, it had become important not to close it down as rumours had suggested might happen, the excellent amount of ground around the buildings had given developers' ideas. To the school the playing fields were a great asset as they were to the developers who viewed the area as a fine housing estate or a splendid block of flats. Now rumours of closing seemed to be dying down and improvement was the operative word. This word had been bandied around ever since the arrival of Maggie Hurst as Head. There had been better exam and sporting results that brought the school to the notice of certain benefactors with material consequences, and then a local footballer (an old boy) took an interest and was hoping to save the playing fields from the developers. Others became interested, the George Pound was now a news item, school dinners improved when another 'local celebrity' took an interest, these were unexpected benefits.

"A snowballing effect," Maggie described it to Annie as more parents became involved in the school activities. A Parent/ Teacher Association was formed and there were many benefits to the school through this, especially when a Gala in the summer proved such a financial success. The weather had been good and everyone enthusiastic.

An ex-librarian Mother offered to *jazz up* the library. Maggie was unsure what this entailed but was delighted when she found pupils there.

"Amazing," Maggie said to Annie, "It's actually being used, I found Raine and Shirley there the other day, they looked guilty, maybe it spoilt their image as rebels but, you never know, they might even open a book."

"It's a pity," replied Annie, "that it needed a murder and mugging not to mention drugs that brought us to the notice of the media." She sighed, "Never again," she told herself.

Things were going well for the school and twinning with a school in a developing country was under discussion.

Annie was still Acting Deputy Head at the George Pound, the school had been promised an energetic young man for the post, the staff looked forward to this event, Annie especially as his arrival would lift many duties from her shoulders. The rumour that he was a science teacher increased her expectations. She herself taught biology but the other science subjects needed an injection of vitality. An energetic young man with ideas? Who knows—with any luck?

Annie wanted more time for her own pursuits, she had put an unhappy and worrying time behind her when her husband, Bernard, had been killed in a car crash, and now with her daughter Sally living with her and a once-had-been-nice bungalow and garden to restore to former—well hardly glory—but to an attractive lived-in appearance with shrubs and colour in the garden and a roof that looked sound. The restoration had been in herself too, she could see how foolish her behaviour had been when, ignoring help and sympathy from family and friends, she had moved into a doubtful and insalubrious neighbourhood. A neighbourhood, she was delighted to see, now partly demolished and considered 'ripe for development'. She still had friends there on the opposite side from her own flat; this side had been left and improved.

Looking forward was better than looking back, she enjoyed her work and her home life, and she had her daughter who had been accepted at the medical school of the nearest University. Sally was taking on all sorts of jobs in order to start off in funds, she didn't want to borrow if she could help it. She would be able to live at home as transport to the town was good.

"But I'd like my own car," she said to her Mother.

"Don't rush it," replied Annie.

Sally had had her 'fling' which included more than she had bargained for. Back-packing around the world, 'doing my own thing' or 'finding myself' was her description and had resulted in a baby that had only lived a few hours.

"Mum, I wanted you so much," Sally cried. "I wanted you but I didn't know it."

Annie was equally sad but happy now in a developing relationship and need of each other. A more mature Sally and a more aware Annie, for Annie had not thought of her behaviour as affecting anyone else, she now thought how selfish she had been especially towards Sally. Her son Joel had a good job in property and could cope but Sally . . .

"You didn't care, you never did," Sally had said. "It was always Dad and Joel."

"That's nonsense."

"No it isn't, Dad was always first with you and then . . ."

"It is nonsense, I'm sorry if you saw it that way, perhaps they needed me more. Oh! Sally, I don't know—but now?"

"Now's different isn't it Ma? Isn't it?"

A pity the way it had come about but yes, now was different.

It was a cheerful Annie that went out to supper with the Hursts on a wet summer evening.

The house was quiet, Lance let her in. Annie realized that she had been 'set up'. She sighed, she might have known that Maggie would not give up so easily. It was obvious that Lance was expecting her and was under the impression that she had come to hear his story. Clever Maggie, she knew Annie too well, and Annie did exactly what was expected of her. Lance was a gentle kind man who enjoyed a quiet life but with an energetic career wife and four boisterous children this wasn't at all easy. He was perpetually surprised at the events that surrounded him and was always unprepared for them. He would have liked his children to be musical but it was obvious to him that their idea of music was quite different from his, although they always listened politely to his efforts to educate them to his tastes. He had given up hope of one of them being a reincarnation of Mozart. Perhaps the youngest, Sam, who everyone said was 'scatty' was hiding his talent and was an undiscovered genius, although such a discovery seemed unlikely, he clung to it.

Annie knew Lance well enough to know that resistance was useless, she accepted a drink and settled herself to listen. He was determined to lay his case before her so she accepted the inevitable along with the drink.

"Perhaps this girl has gone home," she ventured hopefully, trouble at home seemed a reasonable solution.

"She's so musical you see," Lance went on, "some come because they think it's an easy option, not her, not Brenda, she was really good; nobody seems to know anything. Even the police, as you suggest, think she's just gone home."

"Where is home?" queried Annie.

9

"Oh! Kenya, she's a Kenyan girl being paid for by some charity. We have addresses, we've made every enquiry, she's on a special scholarship but everyone is so vague. She's extraordinarily musical and I found her such an interesting character and quite worth the trouble that was being taken over her. Home, Government and charity have all been informed. No-one in college seems to have any idea either, her room-mate said she had a boyfriend in prison but she's inclined to romance but it seems unlikely and no-one took it seriously. Everyone liked her but no particular friend." Lance broke off to refill Annie's glass.

"Are you still seeing him?" he asked.

Annie froze, she was very sensitive about her so-called boyfriend, why did people have to be so nosy, so interfering, and put different meanings into a very ordinary friendship.

"I mean that inspector chap, Neil something or other, are you still seeing him?" Lance went on oblivious of Annie's antagonism.

"I'm not 'seeing him' as you put it, occasionally when he is visiting Dudley and Rose I might be asked over for a meal—nothing more." Annie was calm and hid her exasperation. Lance knew about Dudley and Rose Russell who had been her neighbours when Bernard was alive. Dudley was a special constable and ran his own 'Mr Fixit' business. Rose (the pretty pink variety thought Annie) was a computer wizard.

"I suppose he's a superintendent by now," Lance sighed.

"He may be for all I know, he's a very busy man." Annie tried to be non-committal and uninterested.

There were noises, Annie relaxed, the family were home.

Maggie and Lance had four children, the twins Philip and Jane were taking their GCSEs this year, they were at the George Pound School as were Pat 'coming up thirteen' and her friend Andrew Bushell who was staying with them as his parents were in France. The youngest Hurst, Sam, was still at primary school, he was nine and the image of his Mother. Maggie explained the others away as a 'job lot'

"It's our turn to get supper," said Philip, "I'm afraid it's bought, Mum said it didn't matter just for once, its quiches, you'll have a choice of flavours, okay? There'll be salad, of course."

Annie expressed a liking for quiches and didn't mind if they were bought. The meal was a family affair and everyone hurried to get it ready. The children had been brought up to 'help' and mostly they did this though a certain amount of interfamily grumbling went on.

"I did it last," "It's your turn," "I'm sick of vegetables why can't I have sausages with it." This last was from Sam to Jane who had recently turned vegetarian. "It's dead meat," she assured Sam who said he didn't care, he liked sausages dead or alive.

The parental theory of leading not driving and belief in liberal thinking was good, thought Annie, the Hurst children were taught to express opinions in a logical way, if this didn't always appear . . . well, who knows, they were still young.

Lance tried to get Annie on her own again but she busied herself with the children and laying the table. She caught a glance between Lance and Maggie when Lance gave a brief shake of his head. "I'm sure it was a plot," thought Annie pleased with herself for having avoided a promise to help. "I'm not Miss Marple," she told herself time and time again.

Annie sat next to Sam at the supper table. "Jane's a vegetarian, I get a bit sick of vegetables," he confided to Annie, "I like sausages with mine."

Jane interrupted, "They're dead meat, ground up animals."

"Anyone else a vegetarian?" asked Annie brightly, she didn't want to instigate a family argument just an intelligent discussion, the sort of discussion the parents hoped for.

Only Jane was definite on not eating 'dead flesh', the others hovered; Sam said he was a carnivore. Jane sighed deeply over her family's obstinacy.

Annie tried again, "Are you going anywhere special in the holidays?" she asked.

There was a clamour of hopeful and wild suggestions.

"We can't afford any of these," said Maggie, "you were talking about a computer EACH as you couldn't work out a rota for the one we have. Holidays! Forget it."

"Can't we go back with Andrew? I thought you said we . . ." Pat didn't finish as Andrew interrupted, "It wouldn't cost much to drive over or Dad might fetch me, he said he was negotiating for a sort of farmhousey place on the Brittany coast, or near it, a bit broken-down he said, but plenty of room for tents and barbecues and things—sort of . . ." he looked at the others for support.

"Or you could walk," said Annie, referring, as they all knew, to the time when Andrew, unhappy in France, had arrived by unconventional means on her doorstep in the middle of the night. Her bungalow had been his former home, he had been allowed to stay, temporarily everyone said. He and Pat had been friends since toddler days.

"Dad's done wonders already at that place. There's a huge barn," Andrew looked around the table; he was full of enthusiasm. He had been very unhappy in France but his French was improving, he returned home in the holidays and was beginning to adapt to the idea of going to school there again. His Mother had been a drug addict and life with his family had not been happy.

Annie's interruption was ignored as the family enthused over Andrew's suggestion. Andrew knew he could count on Pat but now everyone brightened and thought of their camping equipment. Lance, not too overwhelmed at the idea, kept quiet.

"What about you?" Maggie asked Annie, "any plans?"

"Not yet, Sally and I are planning a Kenyan trip but I think that it'll be put off until the Christmas holidays. Sally's working all hours, not only to save for the trip but also to have enough so as not to have to get into debt next term. She's talking about bringing Bob as he wants to make aids his specialty but I doubt if he'll be able to come. He's a very steady sort, have you met him? He was at the school before your time I think."

"I met him once with Sally I think, handsome boy, in his third year—medicine isn't it?"

"Yes and he's persuaded Sally to do the same."

"Are we all going?" asked Sam.

"Where to?" asked his father.

"Kenya of course," replied Sam.

"He never listens," said Jane to her twin. "Uh Uh!" Philip was thinking. "Perhaps he's happier that way," he said doubtfully.

Andrew joined in again. "No, you're coming to our place, Dad'll soon start clearing it, it'll be wizard, you'll see."

"Not going to Dorset again then?" Maggie asked Annie, she was still trying to help Lance but was careful not to mention the boyfriend, perhaps one day Annie would confide in her. Annie's so-called boyfriend lived in Dorset.

"Not this time," Annie replied. "Dudley and Rose are going to their special guest house, they asked me to join them for some of the time, they want to show off their baby to their friends Charlie and Renee but I'm not sure I want to be part of an adoring party, though I believe it's a very good baby.

"Where did she get that baby?" asked Sam.

"Sam," said his exasperated Mother, "I've told you all about how babies come."

"Oh! THAT, I didn't believe THAT, you don't fool me; it's not very likely is it? No, I meant which country, where did she get it, you buy them on the Internet. You can get all sorts, that's what I wanted to know." He spoke scornfully.

"They are not sweets," said his father as the others stared speechless and silent.

Annie broke the silence with a return to the topic of holidays. Sam could be safely left to his siblings who were bursting with information.

Annie rather abruptly changed the subject. "Do you know the 'Woodlands'?" she asked of no-one in particular.

"Isn't it a Borstal?" asked Philip.

"Young Offenders," corrected his Father, "I know where you mean." He said to Annie, "No longer Borstal."

"Well, Dudley has asked me to do some extra teaching there, just for August. Someone he knows up there in the education department wants to go on his honeymoon. Another teacher is on sick leave and there appears to be a staff shortage in the remedial section. I've said 'No' because we were thinking of going to Kenya, but as we are now thinking of postponing it, I'm hovering and Sally wants to be here because she says there are so many temporary and available jobs in the summer." Annie paused thoughtfully, "Any extra work I do will only benefit the tax man but I thought it might be interesting and different."

"Will there be elephants?" asked Sam awakening from a daydream.

"In a Borstal?" asked Philip.

"Young Offenders," from his father.

"In Kenya," said Sam, "are we all going?"

The family looked at each other and sighed.

"I was born in Kenya," Annie told them. She didn't think a discussion about elephants was needed at this point. "My father died of malaria and my Mother and I came back. I loved it here but Mother hated it, she returned but I stayed. She died five years ago. I shall enjoy going again and Sally wants to discover her background as she calls it. She's been watching a television programme about finding out who you are."

"About the Young Offenders job," said Lance, returning to the subject of summer teaching.

"I think I'd take it if I were you, what does it consist of?"

"Oh, it's only remedial, three Rs, some can't read."

"Any chance of some music?" Eight weeks of summer holidays was a long time to Lance.

"I don't imagine so," replied Annie sympathetically.

The phone rang.

"I'll answer it," said Andrew, "it'll be Dad, he said he'd ring tonight." His replies to his father sounded excited, though brief.

"He's sending me an IPod," he told them.

"Why can't we . . ." began Philip.

"Just one between us," added Jane quickly.

"I haven't even got a mobile phone," said Sam.

"Tough," said Maggie, "Whose turn is it to wash up?"

"Why can't we have a washing up machine?" Sam asked.

"If you mean a dishwasher, I've ordered one," said Lance. They all stared at him in disbelief, it seemed so out of character.

"I though you said . . ." Maggie looked at him not at all sure if he was serious.

"I changed my mind, now you lot have to decide where to put it."

"Cool," said Philip, "we can move everything round, when's it coming?"

"Tomorrow I think and I don't expect arguments about filling or emptying it, we take it in turns as before. Understood?"

"Cool," said Jane as all left the table to take part in a logical discussion about the best place for this new acquisition.

As discussions often took longer than the tasks Annie was able to leave quietly and without fuss, calling 'Goodbyes' from the front door and leaving the family in the kitchen.

Annie paid a visit to Rose the next morning. It was Saturday and the sun was shining. Victoria Grace (Vicky of course) was two months old and fast becoming the ruler of the Russell household.

Dudley and Rose had new neighbours for the house next door was where Annie and Bernard used to live.

"They've got a baby too," Rose told Annie but they're a bit younger than we are. Sally baby-sits for them too, their baby isn't as good as Vicky, he's six months old and very noisy."

Rose had been horrified when she found she was expecting. The couple were in their forties and had long ago given up hope of a family.

"Of course we didn't bother," Rose said in answer to Annie's raised eyebrows, "Why should we? We've been married for twenty years."

Annie hadn't been sympathetic, just told Rose how lucky she was. She came regularly to admire Vicky, at first she had hated seeing the next-door house in other hands but had now accepted the inevitable.

"I must tell you Rose, I had supper with the Hursts last night and young Sam, in spite of the parents' belief in truth and plain speaking, thought you had bought her on the internet," Annie laughed and was surprised when Rose did not do likewise. She looked serious.

"You'll not believe it but Dud thought the Internet a good idea. He's desperate for a son but didn't want nine months worrying again over me. Do you know Mrs Forster—Audrey Forster?"

"I don't think I do."

Well, you'll not believe this."

"Tell me anyway," said Annie, thinking there was a lot of non-believing to do.

"She pretended to be pregnant and then went over there with a big cushion tied round, I don't know how she got away with it."

"Over where?" asked Annie.

"I'm not sure, I did hear it could have been Romania, it was Eastern Europe. She'd all the papers, said it was British, she'd bribed a lot of people. She'd bought it you see, paid a lot."

"No, I don't know how she got away with it either," agreed Annie. "Sam should be interested. Don't be so silly Rose; it wouldn't be yours. If you want some more go back to Dorset." Annie smiled for she had always insisted that the Dorset air was responsible for Rose's condition.

"Dud wants a boy, if you buy one you can be sure of its sex."

Annie certainly couldn't believe she was hearing this from her sensible friend.

"You might get the right sex but what else? Really Rose, grow up."

There were noises, Dudley came in and with him was Neil LaCoste.

Annie and Neil shook hands, both taken by surprise and both wishing they could be somewhere else and not under the watchful eyes of their friends.

"Have you told Neil?" Annie asked Rose, determined to scotch this scheme irrevocably.

"Told me what?" asked Neil.

Annie sketched out the possible plan, she exaggerated knowing that Neil would understand her anxiety. Dudley was capable of anything.

"You cannot be serious," Neil said to Dudley, "It's out of the question, of course."

"I was only joking," said Dudley, glowering at Rose and Annie. "Aren't they ninnies taking it seriously."

Annie left, if Rose was right and Dudley was considering baby buying it could all be left in Neil's capable hands.

CHAPTER 2

DETECTIVE CHIEF INSPECTOR NEIL LaCoste was a tall, fit, hardworking man in his early fifties, he did not look his age. Annie had Julius Caesar in mind and his description of Cassius *-Let me have men about me that are fat, you Cassius hath yon lean and hungry look, such men are dangerous.* Yes, thought Annie, that's Neil, he is dangerous, heaven help a criminal pursued by Neil.

He was a widower, his first wife having died of cancer but Dudley had told Annie that the marriage had never been a success. "A flighty silly piece," he had said. "Pretty in her way but I never liked her, too flirtatious by far, she turned it on me but I wasn't having any. I didn't tell Neil but I think he knew she was having a go at most of his friends. Mind you," he went on, "I expect he neglected her according to her standards, he's very much the policeman you see, and his job comes first. She liked policemen, I expect a uniform and a bit of . . . well, you know, macho maleness, that sort of thing, so if he wasn't about there were plenty of others. You've got to have a wife sympathetic to the job, someone understanding—like Rose," he finished smugly.

Neil was staying with Dudley and Rose for a few days, he was in the Midlands for longer than this and was looking for a small flat in the town. He met Annie in the Post Office, she accepted his offer of a coffee and took him to a small back street café renowned for its coffee.

"Someone said 'Conkers' was good," he said. "Very good," she replied, "Especially if I want to see half the School and College students. This place is a bit out of the way and quieter."

"I see your point."

They ordered coffee and he told Annie that he was around for a while and was looking for somewhere to live, he did not wish to impose on Dudley and Rose for longer than was necessary.

"I understand," she replied, "they're very busy at the moment, what with the baby . . ." she looked enquiringly at him.

He smiled, "Exactly, a delightful child of course."

"I might be able to help with somewhere to live," she told him. He looked up very hopefully but she shook her head.

"One of our teachers is spending the holidays in France, she and a friend share a small flat, I think I heard that the friend was off back-packing somewhere, do you want me to find out if they want to sub-let?"

"Yes," he said sighing and hiding his disappointment, "and thank you, is it central?"

"Near the police station I believe, a conversion over a betting shop." She was aware of the sigh.

Annie was attracted to him, it was a mutual attraction, they were good friends, Annie was well aware that this was not good enough for Neil, he wanted more but she was determined to remain faithful to Bernard's memory. Her friends waited expectantly.

"In this day and age," someone said, "a man as good looking as that—the past is past, who'd bother."

They drank their coffee in companionable silence. Annie was still worried about Dudley's ideas for increasing his family and she wanted to hear if Neil had squashed any such schemes.

"By the way Rose talked, it didn't sound as if it had been a joke, I expect, in front of you, he had to deny that he was serious. He does have bright ideas and this could have been one of them, can I depend on you?" Annie asked him.

"I'll certainly have another word. At the time I wasn't sure and treated it as a joke, but yes, it isn't very funny."

"Rose said he was considering it as a sure way of getting the sex he wanted and he wanted a boy."

"It's worse than you think, you know, for some Mothers are told that the baby is stillborn instead of which it is sold, some of the midwives are unscrupulous. It's a horrible business, I'll make sure Dudley doesn't get involved in that," he assured her.

Annie told him about Audrey Forster and her cushion.

"I can well believe it," he said, "but I'm quite sure Rose wouldn't agree to such evil trading."

Annie agreed, "Those poor mothers, tell them that story, it will certainly make Rose angry. I suggested that another holiday in Dorset would be a far better way if they wanted another."

He looked puzzled for a moment and then smiled, "Yes, there was something in the air that summer."

He held her eyes for a long time but she turned away, disturbed but still unyielding. After a pause he asked, "May I take you out to dinner tonight. Do you know of anywhere where dining is as good as this place is for coffee?"

"Thank you, yes, and I do know of a fairly new place, Dudley helped to set it up and they welcome new faces. I can tell you news of a possible flat you . . ."

"Can tell you of my progress with Dudley and his baby snatching," he interrupted and added, "Can I pick you up?"

"No, I'll pick you up for I want to see Rose, we can ask them to come with us."

"Do we have to?"

"I know they can't come, Sally is their baby-sitter, they wouldn't trust anybody else and I happen to know she's going to a party tonight."

He raised his eyebrows, "sounds like a conspiracy."

"I must go now," she laughed, "I've work to do, see you tonight."

Annie was beginning to add to her wardrobe, she had felt so uninterested when Bernard had been killed, clothes had been things that covered the body - things you put on in the morning and took off at night, not as she now saw them as an addition to life, to liven up the day and be part of its activities and interests. At the time she had put most of her clothes in store with her furniture. She had now retrieved them and thrown quite a few away, adding new things had helped with her recovery. She had bought a long blue evening gown sometime ago when Dudley and Rose were determined to bring her back to reality. She decided to wear this, it was low cut and the evening was warm.

She rang Rose to ask if she and Dudley could join them.

Rose was disappointed, "Not tonight Annie, Sally can't come tonight, there's no-one else knows our ways. She's going to a party I think."

"Oh dear, so she is," replied Annie innocently.

"Are you going to Chris and Cathy's place?" Rose now asked, "They're doing well, have you booked?"

"No, should I?"

"I'll ask Dud, he'll know. Sorry about tonight. Neil's staying for several weeks so another time perhaps."

Dudley rang back later. "I've booked you in and reserved that little alcove I insisted on when we were setting up the place. Chris will be glad to see you."

Annie thanked him. "See you later," she said. "I'm picking Neil up at seven."

They settled in Dudley's little alcove. Chris and Cathy were indeed pleased to see them, all had been going well, they were beginning to get a good reputation and somehow seemed to think that Annie was partly responsible. "You brought us luck," said Chris.

The food was as good as Annie remembered it, the duck as tasty and the asparagus pancakes perfect and all beautifully served.

"You deserve praise for your knowledge of the district's hostelry," said Neil. "I wonder if . . ."

Annie cut him short, "May I ask you if you are on a case?" she didn't want the conversation to get personal or reminiscent.

"Yes, you may and I am," he became serious now and thoughtful.

Annie waited quietly for him to expand on this.

"I'm still in people trafficking," he told her. "A nasty case in the city, slave labour, you probably heard of it."

"I think so, respectable district, not far from the Synagogue, beauty parlour they called it. I'd wondered if anyone went there legitimately for hair, nails, makeup, anything and if so what did they think."

"Everyone was outraged when they realized, someone had reported suspicious goings-on ."

"I'm not surprised."

"It was another place where illegal immigrants were held, they were all women and had come from—well—all over, from Eastern Europe, Pakistan and even Africa this time. Promised good jobs, you see, and found that they were brought here for prostitution. They have all been interviewed and those implicated in the scandal were arrested. We want to go further afield as before. Who brought them in, who lured them here in the first place and what money changed hands? Modern slave traders!" He was deeply troubled. "It must depress you too," he went on seeing the look on her face, "especially when you were so involved before."

"I wish," she grumbled, "that people wouldn't keep using that word. I was not involved, I had involvement thrust upon me."

"Isn't it the same thing?"

"Not at all."

"So you see I'm here for a while though I may have to go abroad."

"Oh! I nearly forgot, the flat, I'll give you the address. They were delighted, you sounded so safe. It's a pleasant little flat. Helen will be there tomorrow if you want to go and see it."

The sweet trolley arrived but both refused.

"Just coffee for me," said Annie, reluctantly.

"And me," Neil agreed and to Annie he said, "Sorry I can't say let's go back to my place," sighed Neil.

"I'll take you back to Dudley's, don't forget it's still term time and I have work to do."

"You always will have I expect."

Annie ignored this.

"Have I told you that Dudley has suggested I spend some time at the 'Woodlands' during the summer holidays. Apparently they're desperately short-staffed, some ill, some away. I said I might, what do you think?"

"I'm flattered you're asking me."

"Financially it'll hardly benefit me—more tax—but it might be interesting and I could do part time. Sally will be working as we're saving to go to Kenya in the Christmas holidays.

"Fairly tame lot up there, I believe, but don't be too sympathetic, they'll all tell you they were innocent of whatever crime they are supposed to have committed and some of those are quite awful. I don't think you'll come to any harm at the Woodlands. I might pay you a visit, there's someone up there I might want to interview. I'm quite interested in his story."

"Not getting soft are you," said Annie rudely, "interested in what way?"

"Just some information I want, that's all, better from the horses' mouth."

"I think I shall go, I don't have to stay if I don't like it."

"Exactly. Did you say you were going to Kenya?"

"Yes, I was born there and have never been back. Sally wants to research her roots."

He was silent again.

They finished coffee, Neil paid the bill after Annie's protestations of equality.

"I asked you out," he told her firmly, "and you are driving me home."

She left him at Dudley and Rose's after reminding him of his arrangement to see Helen's flat.

"Don't worry about Dudley's baby ideas," he said. "I'll scotch that, I promise you."

"Thank you," she said, "and thank you for the evening, goodbye," she drove off.

Annie went to visit an old friend, old in years not in the length of time she had known him for Alf lived opposite, on the other side of the road to the flat Annie had recently vacated. She had been miserable there but would probably have been miserable anywhere as she had sold her own happy home when her husband had been killed. She had found herself unable to cope and had moved to an unsuitable, depressing place where she could wallow in peace. At the time she had been quite unaware of Alf's existence, on the other hand he had been watching her and knew all about the goings-on at No. 22. This side of the street where he had lived was not being demolished.

Annie had made Alf's acquaintance at the very end of her time there and regretted her former self-pitying behaviour, here was an old man, housebound and living alone, and she had been completely oblivious of his distress.

He welcomed her now as an old friend. "It's all a bit murky—dusty like," he told her, "but they've got some very fine plans for that waste bit at the back. It'll be a big estate, perhaps some nine bungalows for the elderly, though I'm fine 'ere now. Just look over there, it's better than the telly sitting 'ere I can tell you. We've bin gentrified, that's what they call it."

Annie agreed that it would be fine, on Alf's side of the street there was now a space for a small garden or a car, the demolished side, where Annie had lived, would now let in more light and the view would be the new estate. How Alf would enjoy that, thought Annie, as she went to put the kettle on.

A white van now drew up onto the car space and the downstairs tenants came in and shouted up the stairs.

"You okay Alf, who's with you—the social is it?"

"No, it's me," said Annie, "Alf says to come up, we're just having a cuppa."

Bert Harper, plumber and handyman was followed by his very large son Kevin who was still at the George Pound School.

Bert and Kevin had lived briefly in Annie's flat across the road but when the demolition started they moved over. Bert owned a house in another part of town but his wife's sister, who had looked after him and Kevin after the death of Bert's wife, had nagged him into ill health. Bert was a new man now and well liked for he had often done odd jobs for the tenants of this row of houses.

Annie had brought a cake with her; Kevin's eyes lit up, it was his favourite.

"I see they've got a missing girl there up at the college," remarked Alf through a mouthful of cake.

Annie froze. How had Alf got hold of this bit of news, by what means had the news reached him—Bert or Kevin perhaps? She thought it was hushed up. She looked questioningly at Alf.

"It's in the paper," he said. A funny noise came from him, he was laughing. "You had one extra last time, now you've lost one, you'll have to get busy again Mrs B."

Annie was about to put him right and to protest that it was nothing to do with her when Kevin intervened. "If you want any help Mrs Butcher, you will let me know?" he asked hopefully.

Kevin wanted to be Annie's 'sidekick' but as she now told him gently and firmly, "It isn't anything to do with us at the school and nothing at all to do with me, so I don't need help Kevin. Look what happened last time - our interference got you mugged, not a happy experience, kept you off the football field for weeks."

Kevin was not satisfied and sat gloomily regarding her, only the cake kept him moderately cheerful. He was determined on a career in the police force, he felt that any experience was worth the forwarding of this, he was convinced of Annie's infallibility as a detective.

"Everyone seems to think," Annie continued, "that it was my show and I'm turning my back on any schemes to push me into something else."

She was beginning to think that her denials were getting monotonous so she changed the subject.

"How's Aunt Ag," she asked, bringing forth from the others some outspoken epithets.

Annie stopped this outburst by asking Alf if he had any other interesting news. As usual his answer surprised her, where did he pick up his tidbits.

"I hear you're going to that Woodlands place in the summer, better watch yerself up there."

Kevin looked startled, "I suppose it's alright for you up there?" he asked.

"Of course it's all right Kevin, I've told the police and the teachers are well looked after."

"I wish I could come with you."

"Well, I suppose you could if you tried hard enough."

"Oh, I see, joke, I hope," he replied, laughing.

"I was up there for a time," said Bert, "teaching a bit of plumbing, not qualified though so they threw me out. I liked it, some of the lads not half bad."

"You might hear some interesting things there," Kevin said hopefully to Annie.

"I doubt it," she answered, "I'm there to teach and teach is what I'm going to do."

"That's right," put in Alf, "they'll be better criminals if they can read and write."

"And add up," said Bert, winking at Alf.

"Leave it," said Annie.

"I think," Kevin spoke thoughtfully, "I have a feeling that Titch's older brother is there. I went to see if his Mum needed any help but she had a man there who said 'No thanks' in a very threatening way. I didn't mean any harm—just asking like, so I left, but I did have a feeling that all wasn't well."

"Don't worry Kevin. They've been looked after I'm sure." Annie wasn't going to be drawn into the Millar family's troubles. She felt that Kevin should be thinking of his exams now in progress at school.

Help with his studies, yes. As she left she assured him that, if there was anything, he knew where she lived.

They waved her off as they finished off the cake.

That summer continued wet, the grounds became waterlogged and tempers raged. Mrs Gupta, (Maths and occasionally Indian Cookery) beamed on everyone, she loved rain and started, with Maggie's permission and to everyone's delight, some extra-curriculum cookery classes. She took little notice of Caroline Boots whose job it was legitimately. Caroline complained bitterly but Maggie only said, "You could help her." To Annie she said, "Thank God for such as her," for there was no doubt Mrs Gupta's cheerful acceptance and determined example made the others forget grumbles and think of indoor activities on the endless wet days. All looked forward to end of term and the various activities that usually took place in the summer term.

Maggie had a bright idea. "Why don't we start a drama club," she suggested on one particularly gloomy day, "We'll form them into groups, they can write their own plays." To the school she said, "If a group is really good the local television might be interested."

"I only said might," she told the staff as her suggestions activated many theatrical ambitions and the project was a great success.

When the sun came out at last and the grounds dried up an outdoor theatre was constructed. "Better than Shakespeare," one pupil was heard to declare when all the plays were acted in front of the rest of the school.

The winning play was presented at the parents' summer fund-raising event.

All cheered up and the holidays began.

So you're really going to the 'Woodlands', said Maggie, "I'm surprised. Don't get over-tired, it should be interesting, so let us know."

"If I don't like it I shan't stay," Annie reassured her friend.

"Good for you. I see he's here again, that Neil. What a bit of luck."

"For whom?"

"Well, Lance knew you'd help."

"I thought I made it clear I wasn't helping," Annie protested, "but I'll mention it, he may know about it anyway as he's in touch with Inspector David, you must remember him."

Maggie did and later told Lance optimistically that all was in hand. They were all off to France anyway, and her optimism extended to Lance's forgetfulness once he was organizing his family's get-away.

"Let's get this show on the road," was his favourite cry as he tried to fulfill his dream of everybody being ready on the right day and at the right time. They were off at last and Annie busy in her garden, occasionally helped by Dudley and Kevin managed to put out of her mind the incident of the missing girl.

CHAPTER 3

WHY AM I DOING THIS, thought Annie, as she approached the 'Woodlands'. She had expected an open country type of building but it was a grim grey place built originally as a mental home and only in use owing to the large number of young offenders. It had been taken over temporarily as there was nowhere else to put them. She remembered vaguely that it had been known as the 'Mad House', a term fortunately long forgotten, it was now 'them up there', and the Young Offenders Institution. Not a tree in sight and not much wood, thought Annie dejectedly as she approached the gate. 'Up' yes for the 'Woodlands' was nearly at the top of a hill overlooking the river. If nothing else, Annie thought, the inmates then and now have a wonderful view across the valley. Perhaps once there had been trees here.

The Officer at the gate was friendly. "We expected you - Mrs Butcher isn't it?" he looked down at his list. "Mr Best will be pleased to see you. Mr Granville is on holiday, Miss Cartright is ill, has been off for weeks, and I don't know what happened to Mrs Good. Too good for us perhaps," he laughed at his joke. "So you'll be welcome. Bin teaching long?"

"Nearly twenty years," replied Annie, glad to see a friendly face.

"You'll be okay then. I'm Harry—see you in, and see you out, that's me." He pointed the way. "Through that door over there, across the yard, there's a lot going in now, do you see? That's Mr Best's lot."

Annie thanked him and made her way to the opposite block, she met up with Mr Best at the door that had been pointed out to her and she followed him into the education department.

"Good of you to come," said Mr Best. He was a big, heavy man who spoke in the sort of voice that Annie felt should come from a man of his build. Impressive, which, she felt, stood him in good stead with these restless young men. "Shall I be able to cope," she asked herself and told herself not to be so silly, anybody who could cope with a large class at the George Pound would be equally able to manage the six however unruly that Mr Best was detailing to follow her. Their destination was a small study room that looked like two of the previous inmates 'cells' knocked into one.

Mr Best handed out books and folders, "Marked, with his name, and they know what they're doing, no trouble mind—now Fox, you go Jones, Young, McPherson, Millar and Walker, he's new so new folder—here."

Annie took all that he offered, I'll soon get to know them—Fox yes, he looks it, Jones—Welsh by the sound of his voice, Young—yes too young, a fair boy in contrast to McPherson who was very black, probably West Indian. Millar, now where had she seen him before, he winked at her, um-er not a good beginning. Walker continued to stand, towering menacingly over her. The others sat in accustomed places.

"Sit down," she said to Walker as he continued to glower at her.

"Why am I here?" he asked.

"Because you didn't pass the test, when you do you can go on to the other duties."

Dudley had told her the system before she came.

"There's nuffink wrong wif me maffs," he grumbled, still standing.

"Have you got piles?" she asked him.

"Wot?"

"I thought you must have piles and can't sit."

He sat, the others giggled and she went round the class settling, correcting and encouraging. The hour passed quickly.

Another six and again another and the morning was over.

Millar worried her, he got on with his work and was no trouble but he obviously felt she was a friend—curious that. Millar? Was he perhaps at school? She couldn't ask Maggie who was away and was comparatively new anyway but she could ask Alison Beale, the school secretary, she would be able to consult the records. Millar? I feel I should know the name.

Before she had time to consult Alison, the lad Millar came to her, one difference she had noticed was that he called her Mrs Butcher while the other lads said 'Miss'.

"Should I know you?" Annie asked him.

"I was at the school—well—for a bit like, but you were good to young Timmy, thought the world of you he did. He liked school, mostly went for the dinners. That Kevin, remember him do you? That Kevin looked after him."

He turned to the class. "Me brother was murdered," he told them proudly.

They looked at him in awe and then turned to her.

She nearly said, "I didn't do it," for she felt that her name, instead of relating to her dissections now had a different interpretation. There was no giggling over it here.

But Timmy? Of course - our 'Titch' - Timothy Norman Millar who met such a sad end.

When Annie was home she gave Alison a ring.

"Leave it to me," said Alison, "Another Millar? I'm sure we've had several." I seem to remember an Estelle was it, did reasonably well but went off, left home and the district."

"I remember her, not too bad was she? Took a typing course, the eldest of many I think. I'll look through the records and let you know. You say he's up there. What for, did you ask?"

"No, I'm there to teach not to judge, I don't think there are any violent offenders there. Thank you."

"No trouble, I'm still putting an hour or two in school sorting things out. I'll ring you tomorrow when I've found something, okay?"

Annie found herself enjoying the work and by the end of the week told Dudley that she was glad she had decided to go.

"They're no trouble," she said. "Some stupid enough to mess up the test paper probably regret it when they find themselves back in school. Now they're anxious to pass and do something else."

"They get more pay on other duties, they don't get much in education."

"Pay?" Annie exclaimed.

"Why, yes, enough pocket money to go to the canteen and buy fags, rizlas, shampoo perhaps."

"Rizlas?" Annie queried.

"Cigarette papers, a bit of tobacco goes a long way, a fag end makes a whole new fag."

"I'm learning!" said Annie.

Mr Best (call me Arthur) said, "You're doing fine, any chance of your coming here permanently?"

"No, I'm very happy at the George Pound and I love my own subject."

"Pity, could you come full time now?"

"No way,"

"It's Maths," he said encouragingly.

"I might do one afternoon, I'll think about it."

One morning Millar lingered; up to now Annie had been fairly abrupt with him, she didn't think he was there to chat. She had promised that she would see his Mother, "she doesn't come to see me," he had said sadly.

Annie knew that Mrs Millar had a man there, Kevin had tried to see the family without success, the father was in prison in the North somewhere.

"When you see her, tell her I'm fine, foods good, I'm putting on weight, might get into the garden—a good job that."

Annie was surprised that there was a garden in this grim place but agreed it would be a good job and leading somewhere.

On the morning that he tried to stay behind she thought that once again he wanted to talk about home, she was wrong, he had other things on his mind. The officer on duty told him to hurry up, looking resentfully at Annie.

"Sir," said Millar, "Mrs Butcher used to teach me at my old school and I need to discuss my young brother," he spoke with righteous indignation.

"I'll give you three minutes," said the officer remembering that a member of parliament was expected shortly on a visit.

Annie nodded her agreement while thinking that truth was not one of Millar's strong points.

"I don't want to talk about Tim." He said when the officer was organizing the change of class and withdrawn out of hearing. "There's a friend of mine here, Paul Kimani, he's a Kenyan," he now had Annie's full attention, "I really believe him, he's not the sort to invent things, I told him about you and he doesn't mind my telling you. He's my cell mate see, I didn't like going in with a black but he's ever so clean, doesn't smell or anything."

Annie was about to protest but instead she said, "Hurry or your time will be up, three minutes wasn't it?"

"Its lucky you were sent up here, everyone knows about you. Paul does Maths, could you do his class, see him, like?"

Annie waited patiently.

"He said he saw his girlfriend, Brenda, being pushed into a car, being kidnapped he reckoned, he's up here on a put-up job because he saw . . ."

"Times up," shouted the officer.

"You'd better go," said Annie, upset and bewildered. Brenda? Did he say Brenda, she asked herself. "What have I let myself in for?"

The next class came in.

At the end of the morning she found Mr Best in his office.

"I'll do an afternoon of Maths if you like."

He handed her some lists with names. Yes, Kimani, there it was on a Tuesday.

"Tuesday would be the best for me."

"Tuesday it is, perhaps you'd do another as well . . .?"

"I'll see," said Annie as she left.

On the way home she thought, 'what have I done? I couldn't leave it, I have to know. Brenda and a Kenyan, it can't be a coincidence. Could I just forget the whole thing; I could fall ill, have urgent business and not go back at all, I only went because Dudley wanted to help his friend, I don't have to go. Lance will be back, I can tell him or Neil.'

She slept badly.

There were more in the Maths class than in remedial. Paul Kimani was among them. She settled everyone down amid enquiries of, "Got any fags Miss," and, "Can you bring anything in?"

"Nor take anything out and I don't smoke. We have a limited time here so we'll just get on as fast as we can," Annie had no intention of getting into any discussions or involved in any doubtful schemes.

She liked Paul Kimani, his dark eyes were full of hope, she felt guilty for there seemed little she could do.

One Tuesday afternoon Mr Best said, "We've a visitor coming, hopes to see one of yours. That okay by you? There's a small room just opposite your classroom and the Governor thought it the best place for this little chat.

"Who?" Annie began.

"That Kimani, Kenyan lad, I've no idea what its about."

Annie had meant 'who is coming' but she didn't pursue the subject although she did have some suspicion. Her suspicions were correct.

"This is Superintendent LaCoste," said Mr Best with a sideways wink at Annie, "he wants to see Kimani, is that okay by you?"

He was trying to be formal so she didn't say, "Have I any choice?"

She shook hands with Neil and said stiffly, "How do you do."

"Paul," she said to Kimani, "There's someone to see you."

Neil smiled at her and went off with Paul. When he returned Paul said, "He wanted to know about Brenda and, do you know, I think he believed me." He was much more cheerful, looked grateful at Annie, sure, as Millar had told him, that she would sort it all out.

Neil murmured "See you later," to Annie as he left after politely thanking her.

When he had gone Mr Best said, "Had you met him before?" with a hint of disbelief.

"Do you come from round here?" Annie asked resenting his tone, "If you do you will remember that last year the school where I teach, the George Pound, was mixed up in a bit of trouble. He was in on the case and yes, I did meet him and he remembered. He was only an Inspector then, I had no idea of his promotion." She spoke coolly, trying not to remember, it was still very much on her mind.

"Yes, I do remember, there was a local heroine bit wasn't there," he laughed, "Was that you by any chance?"

"It was exaggerated of course, you know the media. Luckily it was all soon forgotten." She knew this wasn't true, she spoke as casually as she could and changed the subject.

Before going home Annie decided to go and see Rose. It was tea time and she knew she was always welcome. To herself she admitted that she hoped either Dudley or Neil would be there, she wanted to hear some background news about Neil's visit. They were all having tea in the garden, the baby Victoria Grace slept peacefully. She was welcomed and tea poured.

"Was it about Brenda?" she asked Neil.

"I think so, I'm trying to fit it into the picture."

"Did you believe him, he said you did but you told me not to believe all I was told."

"It's a peculiar story but Inspector David was worried, this lad was arrested for a supermarket robbery, he swore he hadn't done anything but he had no alibi. Witnesses swore he had done it. These witnesses had nice, clean tidy hair, white boys all terribly respectable, too respectable according to David. They'd all seen him there and he came up before a racist magistrate, a Mrs Daniels, do you know her?

Most seem to," he went on, "and are very wary of her. No chance against all those witnesses, all shopping for their Mothers or so they said."

"I gathered some of this from Paul, I believed him, though I thought he might be hood-winking me. Strangely the other lads believed him. One lad, Millar, the older brother of the murdered Titch, was determined I should hear his tale."

"Even stranger, all those nice clean witnesses have disappeared."

"Distinctly fishy," put in Dudley.

"In my view witnesses are often unwilling, not tidied up and spoon-fed. Inspector David was right to be suspicious. How did anyone know Mrs Daniels would be on the bench?"

"And then?"

"He was given six months in custody, it had been suggested that he was a hardened case but the police said not and it was a first time. They were not happy."

"The story he told me was that he felt he was framed because he saw Brenda pushed into a car. He said he ran away but he was seen. His main worry was what he thought of as a cowardly act but he said there were too many of them," Annie informed him.

"We have an angle on this too, we think we know where she is, but we can't hurry, we need to get all the culprits."

Annie had to be content with this as the baby awoke and the usual adoration began.

"What happened about the baby buying?" Annie asked Neil when both parents had left the table to go over to the pram in the shade of the trees.

"Thankfully all forgotten."

Annie also visited Alf, Bert was there but not Kevin.

"How's it going?" asked Bert. "Up there."

"Interesting," replied Annie.

"Is young Millar still up there?" asked Alf. Where did Alf get his news, here he was confined to the house and yet . . .

"Yes, he was in my class."

"Teaching 'im to read, eh!"

Annie nodded.

"Good, he'll do better next time. He was in that big store break-in, couldn't read so took all the wrong things, then went out of the 'IN', couldn't see the difference between that and the 'OUT'. He didn't get far, not very bright, takes after 'is Dad."

Bert said, "I used to give them fags, you're not supposed to but it kept 'em quiet. One lad had 'is shampoo stolen, what do you think he said?"

"I imagine that he thought it couldn't happen there, stealing off each other."

"You're right and I said that types in there would steal off their own grandmothers and wouldn't worry about the other blokes."

"But some of them do begin to think and I was pleased with Millar, he did someone a good turn. I didn't expect that."

Kevin came in, he put the kettle on and Annie left before she became involved again in talk of crime.

On Tuesday afternoon Mr Best joined her, accompanied by a large surly looking youth, he said, "How many have you got in here?"

"Twelve," replied Annie, this was a larger class than her remedial group and the room had probably been a dining room.

"Then another would make it?" he hesitated.

"Thirteen," Annie didn't sound encouraging. She didn't much take to this newcomer.

"This is Green," Mr Best indicated the surly youth.

Green looked round the room, gave Annie a dismissive look, strode over to Kimani and spat in his face saying, "You black f . . .ing bastard, I'll . . ."

"Out," said Annie. "I'm not teaching him." She found a tissue for Paul.

Mr Best followed Green and put his hand out to restrain any further aggression. Green felt for his knife and finding he no longer possessed one struck Mr Best and floored him.

Annie pressed her emergency bell, officers arrived quickly, Green struck the first to arrive, then reinforcements rushed in. Mr Best was helped to his feet, his nose was bleeding. Annie handed out more tissues. Green was removed, the class was unexpectedly quiet.

Mr Best looked at her, "You'll do," he said snuffily, "No panic."

"None at all," and to the class, "Books open—plenty of work to be done." She was surprised at their docility, perhaps they were pleased that, for once, they were not the central figures.

"That's 'Big Mouth' that was," said one, "We'll not see him for yonks."

"Got any fags Miss?" said another.

"That was one of *them*," said Kimani. At this point the duty officer arrived, "Governor wants to see Kimani, okay by you?"

"Yes," said Annie distractedly. '*One of them*' he had said.

Now she had something to tell Neil.

On Thursday Mr Best informed her that Paul Kimani had gone. "That Superintendent came and they took him away."

"I think," said Annie, "that there was something in his tale!"

"Maybe, you can never be sure."

'*That was one of them*' was still in her mind. Neil was pleased, and she was pleased at his reception of it.

"It fits in, we really may be onto something at last."

"My last week at the 'Woodlands', I shall be glad to get back to the George Pound, at least it was built to let the light in.

"I finish tomorrow," she told Mr Best. He sighed heavily.

"Pity," he said, "You're few and far between."

The Hursts were due to return. Sally found a welcome home banner in a new shop selling 'almost everything'. Between them they put this up, Annie picked flowers and they cooked pizzas, quiches and many tempting bits and pieces. This, with a bottle of wine, cheered the jaded travelers, all anxious to tell of their wonderful holiday.

"And how was yours?" Maggie enquired.

"Interesting," replied Annie.

CHAPTER 4

ANNIE'S OCCUPATION WITH THE YOUNG offenders along with essential work in her garden had led her to neglect her swimming programme. She now started again, hoping to meet up with her friend and swimming partner Sergeant Tracy Williams. Tracy was a very keen swimmer.

The pool where they used to meet was some distance from the town, Annie went there hoping not to meet half the school as there was another pool nearer to the town where she knew that the school swimmers met. Further afield was this much bigger Leisure Centre with facilities for those keen on all sorts of exercise. This included Tracy who, inclined to put on weight, also visited the gym.

"I must keep my figure," she told Annie, "I don't want to be called plump."

"You're just right," replied Annie, "you've a great figure."

She was there when Annie arrived, viewing herself in a mirror.

"Still worried?" Annie teased her.

"I think I was chosen for this job because I've what I heard spoken of as a 'comfortable figure', I don't know, what do you think?"

"What's the job, or can't you tell me?"

"I don't mind telling you, seeing who you are."

Annie bit back "who am I", and said instead, "It sounds very mysterious, not dangerous I hope."

"It's a bit hush-hush and Inspector David was worried but he consulted with Superintendent LaCoste who thinks it might work."

"Intriguing, tell me more, that is if you can."

"To you, yes. It's a bit depressing, I'd like to talk about it."

"Let's have a coffee."

They went to the pleasant café, there were tables, chairs and bright umbrellas outside, and through open doors the smell of coffee reached them. "I'll have mine black," said Tracy, Annie made no comment when her friend chose a large cream cake.

"Well," said Tracy, "I had to do some dressing up as a rather coarse, yucky character and then I was sent to an equally scruffy pub, not my sort at all. This woman they wanted me to make friends with went there regularly, they knew that much, probably a madam." She looked at Annie, "You know what I mean, they thought she was running a brothel. Again it could be women brought in illegally for the sex trade," she paused, "We do get caught up in this don't we?"

Will someone tell everyone that I'm not caught up in anything, thought Annie despairingly. I can't even come for an innocent relaxing swim. She said nothing, however, and encouraged Tracey with a smile.

"They wanted someone on the inside and I had to pretend I wanted a job, it wasn't easy because this woman, her name seems to be Buffy, didn't talk much, and she still doesn't."

"You got the job then, is Buffy a nickname?"

"I've no idea. Yes, I got a job in the kitchen, I try to be as unpleasant as she is, grumpy, taciturn, that's me."

"That'll need some acting!"

"I was always good at acting at school. I don't mind that bit but Buffy is a horrid woman, she's not the boss, she only runs the kitchen and doesn't talk except to say 'Do this, do that'," Tracy finished her coffee and cream cake, she went for another. When she returned she said, "I'm glad I chose the police force."

Annie couldn't see the relevance of this but she was enjoying the story.

"What then?" she asked.

"We have to catch the boss as well so I have to hang on there to try and make a timetable, such as when these women come and go, my hours don't include this actual moving of the women. They're taken, you see, to other places to—to—we're not sure where we want to catch everybody and I haven't even seen the boss yet."

She paused, Annie put her arms around her, "You're doing marvelously, no need to get dispirited."

"I feel I'm not getting anywhere except in one thing but I haven't told anyone yet."

"Tell me, get it off your chest, everything takes time you know, even in teaching. If you're in the kitchen who is the food for?"

"Breakfast is served before I get there, I clear and wash up the remains, and it's mainly bread and some cheap jam. I help prepare soup, a lot of not very appetizing vegetables go into it, I don't know when they eat it. There's rice too. I cook it with oddments of meat, I expect it's warmed up, I don't know when. It's the tray that worries me."

"Tray? Who's it for?"

"That's it, I didn't know. Buffy puts stuff on a tray and comes back with an empty one, often not touched but yesterday she was busy and handed it to me."

"That's good, she trusts you."

"She said 'upstairs' but I just stood there, I'd never been upstairs. 'Down the passage—end door', she'd something else on her mind, someone had come through the shop."

Shop, what shop? Annie thought. Tracy wasn't telling this very well, she was obviously upset, but a shop had not been mentioned.

"It's only papers, magazines and a few sweets, it's not exciting and it's not always open."

"That in itself sounds fishy."

"So Inspector David says, he called it a front, a sort of fake to hide the real purpose of the premises."

"So you went upstairs, what happened?"

The door was locked, all the doors were locked, and I tried several. I knocked at the one at the end, no answer. It was bolted as well as locked, I unlocked, unbolted and went in. A black girl was in bed, there was no sign of any clothes, I think they'd been taken away. She covered her head but I said 'you okay love?', she uncovered and looked at me as I put the tray down. I gave her the thumbs up, I tried to signal hope, you see. 'Over soon, don't worry,' I said. "I tell you—I'm the one worrying."

"Let's swim," said Annie, "I need to think. A black girl you said, only there's one missing from the college, surely you remember?"

"I had forgotten—oh! Lord!"

"Dr Hurst's student—from the college—now does it come back?"

"You think there's a connection?" Tracy was suddenly Sergeant Tracy Williams, life had come back to her.

"I'm going back to the station. This must be reported in the proper manner. Thank you and thank you again." Forgotten was her depression, she was back on the job, she strode purposefully to the car park, revved up her motorbike and was off.

Annie went swimming.

Kevin came to see Annie, partly because he wanted to know about life at the 'Woodlands' and partly because he was going away for a few days.

"Dad's fine these days so I thought I'd go and see Gran. You remember Gran?"

Annie did, she had made friends with Sheila Nixon when Kevin had been mugged, she was a cheerful, hardworking, helpful grandmother.

"How are you getting there Kevin?" asked Annie.

"I'll hitch, I'm sure I can . . ."

"I'll drive you, I won't stay with you, I'll find somewhere."

"Are you sure?"

"Quite sure, when can you be ready?" She was already mentally packing. Manchester wasn't everyone's idea of a summer holiday but she'd made friends there and it would be a break before term began.

She turned off her mobile, the answers on her house phone could collect for her return.

Kevin returned from Manchester with her, she drove him to Alf's.

"I'd better come in and say Hello," she said, "or he'll never forgive me."

Kevin shouted up the stairs and Alf replied with a 'come on up.'.

"Bin busy again then have you, heard all about it," he chuckled knowingly.

How did Alf get his news—but now—heard all about what?

"We've been up to Manchester, I thought you knew."

"Oh! That, no, I mean the big raid, found your missing girl didn't you. That's why you went away to avoid the goings on, we all know you."

Bert came in at that moment, he joined them and waved his newspaper at them, "You got 'em then, found your girl, well done you."

Annie protested as usual while feeling its uselessness.

"You're joking aren't you, you knew all along, you never let on do you?" Bert and Alf exchanged glances while Kevin stared at her in open admiration.

Annie didn't stay for the expected cup of tea, she left as Bert put the kettle on.

She went straight to the Hursts, they were sitting in the garden, Lance got up and came to her, taking her hand and shaking it vigorously.

"Marvelous", he said, "I knew I could rely on you."

Protestation was useless so she took a vacant chair and sat down as Lance continued, "She's in a safe house somewhere, that nice Inspector David came. It was wise of you to go away while that big raid was on. It made quite a stir."

Maggie said, "We're going to suggest that she comes and stays with us, she can go to college with Lance and we can all look after her." It seems to be true, accept it Annie told herself.

"Have you the room?" she queried.

"Andrew has stayed in France, he's going to try again, his French is much better, and Peter and Sarah both want him home, so room for another."

Lance added, "Brenda's parents are coming over, they want to meet you and Paul of course."

"Where is Paul?" asked Annie.

"He's safe, he may go back with Brenda's people. I expect you'll hear all about it from your Neil," said Lance.

Annie sighed, but said nothing except, "He's not my Neil."

"Lance has been able to see her", said Maggie, taking no notice of what she considered to be Annie's foolish and reluctant acceptance of the inevitable.

Lance took up the tale, "She's a bit shaken, it was a very nasty experience, and she'll be fine with us if the parents agree. She could return to Nairobi with you and Sally if you really are going there for Christmas."

"We really are", said Annie.

Only a few days now to the start of the Autumn Term, the young teachers who had lent Neil their flat had returned so perhaps Neil was back with Dudley and Rose.

Helen Scott was enthusiastic about their sub-let. "He left everything just as it should be and he paid in advance," she told Annie, "he added a bit more at the end for breakages and deterioration. There was only one broken glass and we didn't notice any deterioration. He's gone back to his friends for a bit but he's coming to our party on Saturday. It's a bit of a homecoming—end of holidays thing, you'll come won't you? Sally's coming too."

Annie agreed to come, she would meet Neil casually without having to seek him out. She would hear details of the raid, unavailable to Alf.

The party was noisy, the flat too small for the large number of people invited. Everyone had brought a bottle, some more than one. A large boyfriend, no-one was quite sure whose, had taken over the kitchen, the smell of cooking was invading the rest of the flat, every now and again platefuls of food appeared, some traditional like sausages on sticks and some of unknown origin. All were pronounced excellent by strong minded guests. Sally and Bob looked at each other and disappeared with firm steps and determined expressions into the kitchen.

Annie looked round for Neil, he appeared at that moment at the entrance door.

"Do you come here often?" she asked him as he moved towards the kitchen and handed in the obligatory bottle.

"Frequently", he replied as he returned to her, "Though it never was quite like this."

They both laughed, he seemed in a lighter mood.

"It isn't quite your scene either is it?" he didn't wait for an answer, "When I was living here and to save myself a lot of trouble, I found a useful small restaurant just round the corner, the food's reasonable and their omelets are good!"

"Not much chance of a quiet corner here is there? I'll just tell Sally as I have the only key."

"See you later Mum" was all that Sally said, but she added, "I don't suppose anyone will miss you, they might even be glad."

"I don't imagine we'll be missed," Neil said, repeating Sally's remark. Annie followed him down the stairs, she took his arm in a companionable way as they strolled through the town to his 'useful restaurant'.

"I've made friends here," Neil told her, "We can talk here. I used to find it restful after a hectic day."

"I've heard of the hectic time," Annie said as they settled themselves into a pleasant nook and ordered the recommended omelets, "Can you tell me more?" she added.

"You probably didn't know that Brenda Kimotho is the daughter of a politician who's been fighting corruption. He allows his daughter to come here to study music and what happens . . . it was almost an international incident."

"So that's how you came into it?"

"Inspector David had been in touch with me, he'd been unhappy about the conviction of that boy at the 'Woodlands'—Paul Kimani. All those tidy youths—he thought it was unnatural. All swearing they were shopping for their mothers, he thought it very overdone. Someone knew that a racist magistrate would be on. Doesn't it all sound odd to you?"

"Very odd, I didn't know anything of this until I heard it from Paul by way of the Millar lad. And then you removed Paul, I was glad about that after that great bully spat at him."

"Apparently he'd said, 'its one of them', it was - it was one of the 'Shoppers for Mother' gang. We removed Paul for questioning we said."

"Is he safe?"

"Oh yes, quite safe."

"I'm glad, I liked him, his story rang true."

"Then the whole situation changed when you frightened Sergeant Williams into thinking . . ."

"Annie interrupted, "Neil, how could you, I didn't frighten Tracy, only the story she told me seemed — well, you know . . ."

"And had no right to tell you."

"I agree but everyone thinks . . .," she hesitated, he surely knew that everyone thought . . . thought what? She abandoned thoughts and said, "Go on—she did tell me and I put two and two together."

"She'll have to be moved I'm afraid."

"Tracy—moved— but why? We go swimming together."

"I'm sorry to spoil that but she disobeyed orders. We either wanted her arrested with the rest or well out of it. What do you suppose she did?"

"I can't imagine, I always thought her so disciplined, devoted to her work, unlikely to waver."

"She went in with the force—in full uniform. She so disliked the Buffy woman, she wanted to see the arrest, to get one over on her. She'll be a marked woman, we have to get her away."

"But not in disgrace surely."

"Perhaps not, but not rewarded. She's not against moving, her Mother wants to move to London so we'll make concessions I promise you."

Annie relaxed and laughed inwardly at Tracy's behaviour for who could blame her. "What happened to this character, this Buffy woman?" she asked.

"She was by far more important that Williams thought and it was her son running the 'up front' newsagent. She's in custody, the women held there are all very willing to testify and we may get some of the organizers when the real talking begins. It's a pity we had to go in so soon but given the circumstances it was unavoidable. Some of the stories these women tell are absolutely horrifying."

"And it was Brenda?"

"Yes, indeed, we have your Brenda and I believe her parents arrive tomorrow."

"So Maggie said."

Neil was still thinking of his work, "Even if we do get some of these evil types there will always be someone to take their place. It's very profitable you see."

Annie was silent in sympathy. She changed the subject to try to lift the frown from his face.

"Have you gone back to Dudley and Rose?"

He smiled, "Yes, but I'm on the move anyway. I've let my place in Dorset for six months, it's all a bit vague at the moment."

"Shall we have coffee?"

"Or at your place?"

At that moment they were new and cheerful newcomers. Sally and Bob came in, delighted to see them and, sure of a welcome, joined them.

"We've eaten," said Sally.

"Well, sort of," said Bob.

"Bob said you'd be here so we came for coffee."

"How did Bob know we'd be here," Neil was curious.

"He said he'd often seen you here."

"He should be in the force."

"Have you had coffee?" Sally wanted to know, she looked at the table, "obviously not. It's four coffees then—you get them Bob."

Neil looked resignedly at the table.

"Black for me," he said.

Dr Francis Kimotho and his wife Evelyn arrived in style. They had hired the largest car with driver that was available at the airport and had driven from there. The Hursts were somewhat overwhelmed but Dr Kimotho soon put them at their ease. "We could not possibly accept such generous hospitality, you are so good and we must not spoil this friendship. No, we are not staying with you, we are booked in at 'The Splendid' in town."

He introduced his wife and a young son Simon, who looked hopefully at the family in the background. Sam had gone for a tape measure (as he told them later) to measure the car.

"We will indeed come in and meet your family and tonight you will join us at the hotel for a little celebration. All of the family," he assured them as he too looked at the young people in the background. Simon will have company. Also this Mrs Butcher we hear so much about, she is to be with you without fail."

When they had gone Maggie rang Annie, "You'll have to come, dress up a bit, it look a bit of an occasion. They're interesting people. He was educated at the LSE, London School of Economics not the Stock Exchange. You can talk about your trip there, I'm sure they'll be helpful.

So Annie dressed up a bit, she met Brenda for the first time and accepted, without her usual protestations, their thanks and offers of hospitality on her and Sally's forthcoming holiday.

Afterwards she admitted to some unease. "I think Sally has her mind on something more rugged," she told Maggie, "personally I am not against a certain amount of luxury."

"We shall see," she added.

CHAPTER 5

"YOU'LL BE GLAD TO HEAR," said Maggie, "That Paul is going back to Kenya with the Kimothos. Brenda is going too, but may be back for the Spring term."

She and Lance had dropped in at Annie's for a drink, the occasion being 'end of holidays and back to work tomorrow'.

"Good," said Annie, "He seemed a bright lad to me with a good grasp of math's essentials. I think he only pretended to need maths in order to contact me. Young Millar had given him an exaggerated and glowing report of my influence and capabilities."

"Justified as it turned out," Lance put in smugly.

Maggie laughed, "A reputation now reinforced."

"I can't help that can I? It was just chance."

"Here's to you," said Lance raising his glass, "And young Brenda is safe as well."

"To continue about Paul," said Maggie, "Dr. Kimotho has promised to find him a good temporary job while he looks into the possibilities of a place at Nairobi University."

"I think he has a brother working at the Norfolk Hotel in Nairobi, so he'll have somewhere to live."

"You did say that Kenneth Millar was at the Woodlands?"

"Yes, and I'd like to help if we can when he comes out. With a family like that what chance have any of them?"

Maggie agreed, "I'll find out what I can. Alison is bound to know. We are keeping in touch with Inspector David."

"Perhaps, at the same time, we could find out about Sergeant Williams, Tracy, she said she'd write but you know how it is, people don't always do what they intend to do."

"I heard about that, a pity, uprooting her like that."

"She lives with her Mum who wanted to go so it wasn't all that bad."

"What exactly happened?" Lance wanted to know.

"She let her basic instincts get the better of her."

Sally came in at that moment with some edible tidbits to accompany their drinks.

"Here's to the New Term," said Annie.

"And to you and all you've done for the school," proposed Maggie.

"Me - me? It's you that has done so much!"

"I may have improved things but you've put it on the map. Before it was 'Oh that old place, isn't there somewhere else'?"

"If it was me, it wasn't in the way I should have wanted to 'put it on the map' as you call it."

Maggie ignored this, "I actually heard someone in the town say, 'We're HOPING to get him into the George Pound'—before it would have been—I suppose there's nowhere else."

Sally, having no idea of the topic of conversation said, "Bob can't come."

"Were we expecting him?"

"Not now, I meant to Kenya with us."

Annie, having no idea that he was to accompany them, was momentarily taken aback, she was silent while she rethought the situation. The Hursts, thinking the circumstances probably needed quiet family discussion, finished their drinks and departed with a 'see you tomorrow' and a reluctant look at Sally's offerings.

"Right," said Annie when they had gone, "So Bob can't come, never mind and I'm off to bed." She left the room but almost immediately returned; she sat down and helped herself to the delicious looking edibles that Sally had prepared.

"Any reason he can't come apart from the fact that I hadn't asked him?"

"Oh Mum, don't be like that. Surely you realize that we're a couple."

"Yes, but that doesn't mean . . . does it?"

"Anyway, he can't come, someone important is coming and he's got work to do so that's that."

Annie agreed to this and went to bed.

Tomorrow was the first staff get-together of the term and the new school year.

The staff meeting inevitably started with talk of various holidays, stories and experiences abounded. Maggie brought everyone to order "or we'll be here all day."

Everyone was alert.

"We no longer call it a staff meeting," she told them, "it's a discussion group, the main purpose of which is to welcome new members of staff and talk of how we shall miss those who have left us."

"Or how glad we are to see the back of them," muttered someone furthest from Maggie.

"Hear, hear!"

Maggie frowned, "Okay, whether we do or not." They were all probably thinking of a departed difficult and racist ex-teacher thankfully now retired.

Dawn Johnston-Smith, new last term and oblivious to staff room gossip, stood up, "I think a theme for the term would be a good idea."

"We've got plays and things, not to mention Christmas," said Ceinwen Roberts, mentally singing some carols.

"Christmas—ah—yes."

"In a multicultural society . . . " Adam started.

"What do you mean?" asked Ceinwen, "its still Christmas whatever sort of society it is."

"I thought it was the Winter Festival now," said Adrian, hoping to stir things."

"Rubbish," said Caroline, "Christmas is Christmas."

"We could combine all the activities," suggested Annie, hoping to smooth the Christmas controversy. "A short play followed by the Gala. What do you think?"

"If people don't want to come to the Nativity play we shan't force them," said Dawn Johnston-Smith.

"We'll work everything in," said Maggie, not wishing for a discussion on political correctness, "And now I want to introduce Dan Sleep, our new Deputy Head."

But Ceinwen was still worried, she had already met Dan Sleep and dismissed him as of no use in her musical projects, also she was a sincere Christian, as was Dawn.

"We have to have carols," she insisted, "There isn't any question about it, and a tableau or two to set it all off."

John Durant's replacement, Chris Melby, now joined in, he saw hope as he looked at Dawn, "We could hot it all up a bit," he suggested, "Boom, boom, drums and things, perhaps homemade instruments, I'm hot on the drums . . ." he trailed off with an extra "Boom, boom," and a rattle of his chair back.

Caroline stood, all set for a different approach to anything suggested, but Maggie was before her.

"Dan Sleep," she said.

Dan stood up, he had been sitting at the back slumped down in his chair, he was now seen to be very tall, well over six feet, and his nearly bald head was no indication of his age, he was still in his twenties.

"Hello everyone," he said breezily, "Yes, I'm Dan and I'm looking for somewhere to live, only just arrived, I was at London University and teaching at a school on the outskirts . . ."

"Are you married?" asked Helen Scott, she wasn't particularly interested but thought that everyone should know.

"Not yet," he replied, looking round hopefully as he viewed the potential. He passed over Annie, Caroline and Mrs Gupta but perhaps . . .

Maggie interrupted this self introduction, "Dan is a science teacher as well as our Deputy Head, he is young for this appointment but Mrs Butcher will be able to help him as he will undoubtedly help her."

"I thought Africa would be a good theme," Dawn was not to be put off by irrelevant side-tracking such as a new Deputy Head. Things would probably go on as they always did under Maggie.

"Africa is a big country," said Annie.

"Impossible," said Caroline Boots.

Dan, who had sat down, now stood up again. He's learned to use his height thought Annie, I hope there's more to him than that.

"It could be divided up into countries, classes could each take a different country. I'm not sure how many there are."

"Between thirty and forty," said Sheila York.

"There you are," said Caroline.

"Fascinating," continued Dan, "Some coastal, some desert, forests, riverside, different religions, the Rift Valley . . ." he faltered.

"I'll be there next holidays," added Annie.

"It's a bit of an undertaking," said Maggie, "But all the more reason for tackling it and improving our knowledge."

"We're going to Kenya and we thought," Annie contributed, "that we would look for a school to twin, perhaps one wouldn't be enough."

"I thought the twinning idea was great," said Sheila York, "But how and where do we look for one—but if Annie is actually going there . . ." she broke off in a questioning voice.

"One of the parents, Major Hastings, Sylvie's father, lent me some photos of a school in Nairobi; he seemed to think it suitable. I'll hand them round. The original twinning idea came from Mrs Gupta but we hadn't thought of Africa then." As she spoke Maggie was handing out some beautifully produced computer printouts. The staff looked at them, someone sniffed loudly.

"They aren't my idea of an African school," said Helen Scott, "Look at the way they dress, they put our lot to shame, they haven't looked like that since I've been teaching here."

"They look very nice," said Caroline Boots.

"I agree," Bill Harris was new this term. No-one ever agreed with Caroline. ("Maybe someone wanted to get rid of him!" Maggie said to Annie later)

"I'd thought of something more—well—sporty," said Adrian Lane.

"And I'd thought of something more African" added Ceinwen Roberts.

"Or do you mean what we think an African school should be like," suggested Maggie, "Or used to be like?"

"I think we should wait," said Annie, "And our project should see the continent in terms of its differences, its geology, its geography, commerce, physical features and statistics."

"I like that," said Mrs Gupta, "Commerce, statistics, plenty of scope for practical and applied maths."

"Right," said Maggie, "Give it some thought, we'll let the term get into its stride first, and we'll have a better idea of things then. Next on the agenda is this Gala the parents want to give. It was so profitable last time so I'm reluctant to say 'No'—but—this is the winter term and—inside? What do you think?"

The meeting continued with its usual flow, with its hopes and expectations. It was when Maggie was packing up her papers and beginning her closing words that Mrs Gupta said, "I do not want to be given an African country to study if there is a war on there."

Everyone was alert.

"We none of us want one with a war on," said Caroline apprehensively.

"If there's a war on we won't count it in," said Maggie.

"That should deter them," said some wit with a laugh.

Maggie closed the meeting but discussion continued in groups as the staff left - it was going to be an interesting term.

It was, and, in spite of many pessimistic forecasts, everything went with a swing. Dan Sleep proved to be of much greater assistance than Annie had expected. He told her that he hadn't expected to get the job. "If I make a success of it I might get a headship, I've no commitments to hold me back, you see, I can go anywhere, so what do you think?"

Annie agreed that he had a good future before him.

Dan continued, "I've seen a boy at the school who's bigger than I am, must be a good two inches taller, looks like a rugger player. Is there rugger here?"

"I know the lad you mean, he's very tough and a . . .," Annie tailed off, no she wouldn't or couldn't describe Kevin. Dan would find out soon enough. Now she said, "No, we're not a rugger playing school—yet. Let's think about it, put the idea to Maggie. There's a good amateur club near, cricket too I believe, get in touch with them, why don't you? Keep your eye in as it were. Or you could join in helping with the soccer?"

"Perhaps that big boy would come to the rugger club with me, what do you think?"

"You can but try," Annie replied.

"He might know of somewhere to live," said Dan. "Nobody seems to be of much help. I'd like a small flat but anywhere would do."

"You'll find somewhere, it always takes time to settle in."

Annie thought it wouldn't take him long, he was very confident, he's lucky to be working under Maggie. The old head, Mrs Witherspoon, would have been no support, rather the reverse, and by no means encouraging. He may be wet behind the ears but he'll make it eventually.

"I expect he'll be pleased to be asked," said Dan confidently.

A few days later Kevin came to the bungalow, "Could you come and see Alf, he misses your visits, and says its ages since your last time."

"I've been so busy Kevin, tell him I'll come at the weekend, and say I'm sorry but what with the bungalow and school—he'll understand. I'll see him on Saturday. Is all well there?"

"Everything's fine thank you—see you then."

Alf was jaunty when she called.

"Going to Africa I hear," he said.

"Only for a holiday, it's not permanent," replied Annie.

"Glad of that—nasty place—I see it on the telly, snakes and all those animals eating each other."

"Talking of snakes," put in Kevin.

"What about them?" Alf wanted to know.

"Kevin turned to Annie, "Did you know that Mr Sleep kept snakes?" he asked her.

"No wonder then that he can't find anywhere to live," Annie smiled at him.

"He asked me if I knew anywhere."

"And do you?"

"Oh, yes, I sent him to Aunt Ag's but I told him to keep quiet about the snakes."

"Kevin, you're wicked."

They all laughed.

"She's been looking for a lodger for some time and he wasn't happy where he was. I was only being helpful," Kevin grinned, "I'm afraid she found them and he's lent them to a Zoo."

"Pity he couldn't send her there too," said Bert.

The term was well away when the subject of the African project was brought up again. Annie and Sally had been pouring over every book on Kenya that they could find. Annie hoped to be allocated this country when the draw, organized by Alison, took place. Caroline Boots drew Nigeria, "Of all places!" she grumbled.

"Aren't you lucky," Alison reassured her in her usual cheerful way, "No war there, lovely and warm, so interesting, lucky you."

Alison repeated something of the sort to everyone, she cheated enough to ensure that Annie had Kenya. "What a coincidence," she said, "When you're going there."

Maggie said, "I've never seen so much interest in maps before, we'll continue this into the Spring Term."

"It is good," said Mrs Gupta, "Especially for those who thought that India was part of Africa."

Half term seemed to be there almost before term had begun.

"We'd better postpone the project until next term, what do you think?" asked Maggie to the staff. Everyone was noncommittal but when they returned from the brief holiday she was voted right.

"Better to postpone it," said Mrs Gupta and not rush it and spoil it."

After half term everyone was glad of this wisdom, what with the Gala in the main hall, rehearsals for the plays and the usual Christmas bustle, the African activities remained in the classrooms where parents could visit and be told by their excited offspring how, 'one day', it was all going to be put together.

"Dan Sleep settled down at last," Maggie said to Annie on the last day of term, "It took him time but I hear he is fairly active in the town. He goes to the gym with Dawn, to 'Conkers' with the group that gathers there, to the pub with some college staff and even to tea with Mrs Gupta. Lance says one of the younger lecturers there has asked him to share a flat next term; apparently his present landlady is a bit of a nag. Always comparing him unfavourably with her wonderful nephew."

"I don't believe this," replied Annie, "This nephew couldn't do anything right."

"Really," said Maggie, "Dan kept snakes, did you know?"

"I think he's given them to a Zoo," said Annie hopefully, "I don't want them in the lab. I'm glad he's settling down, not so much that he is waiting for your retirement, but just quietly looking to the future somewhere else."

Relaxing at last after the terms' excitements Annie watched Sally pack. Bob drove them to the airport.

Sally wandered off to look for a trolley.

"It's too late now," said Bob, "But I wish I was coming with you. I've just so much to do though, so much work, I'm sorry!"

"It would have been great to have you with us Bob. Maybe another time?" Annie replied.

"You'll look after her won't you?"

"I've been doing that off and on for years . . . except," she added, "for one brief period."

"She told me all about that, you know, that's why I'm so anxious, it was a bad time for her."

Sally returned triumphant and sparkling. "I wish you were coming Bob."

"So do I," they clung together for a moment.

"There'll be a next time," said Annie.

They joined their queue.

We really are here, thought Annie, waiting for our flight to Nairobi to be called.

CHAPTER 6

ANNIE COULDN'T ACCOUNT FOR HER feeling of depression as they moved towards passport control. She looked at Sally who was glowing with anticipation. 'It's just me,' thought Annie, 'I'm, tired, and I haven't the happiest memories of life here.' A hand came out for her passport and a friendly grin cheered her.

"Teacher," he said, "That's good, I should like to have been a teacher. Do you still teach?"

"Yes," replied Annie, thinking 'this is hardly the time for a meaningful discussion.' "Yes," she repeated, "I still teach. Do I look that old?" He smilingly returned her passport and they passed through.

They changed some pounds into Kenyan shillings and went outside to look for a taxi.

"Is there a special one for The Norfolk?" asked Sally as they looked about them. Then Annie spotted Dr Kimotho coming towards them with outstretched hands.

"I enquired at The Norfolk, they are expecting you there, and they knew what time you were arriving and thought you would be on this plane."

"We were looking for a taxi," said Sally hopefully.

"I will be your taxi. Now tell me, do you want to go straight to the hotel or will you come home with me and have whatever meal it is to you?

"I think its breakfast," said Annie, "But if you don't mind I think the hotel first, we haven't slept much and we started off tired. Thank you very much for the lift, perhaps we could come to you another time."

Dr Kimotho agreed, "Tomorrow perhaps. My wife is so much looking forward to meeting you, and Brenda is at home at the moment."

"Thank you," said Annie again, "Tomorrow it is."

He left them at the hotel where more welcomes awaited them. Paul Kimani's brother Leonard was an Under-Manager here and Paul was there ready to tell again history of former troubles and rescue."

"Leonard says I can stay awhile and help you when you need help."

"Have you a job here?" asked Annie.

"Not yet," he replied, "But I sort of help a bit."

He took their luggage to their rooms and offered to show them round.

"We're okay for the moment," said Annie, and when he had left she said to Sally that she hoped he wasn't going to be a nuisance.

They unpacked, found swimwear and went to look for the pool.

Paul proved to be unobtrusively helpful; he brought them snacks around the pool and told them of mealtimes before quietly retiring and leaving them to it.

It was cold and wet when they left England so that the warmth and the sun surprised them, the contrast was so great. It enveloped them and Annie found that her depression had completely left her.

"We may get sick of sun," Annie told Sally.

"Never," replied Sally, "And just look at all the fabulous colour, why, even the soil is red."

"All the same, we'd better not get sun-burnt too soon," Annie warned. "If we get to the coast . . ."

"What do you mean 'IF'?" said Sally, "There's no 'if' about it, of course we're going to the coast."

Next morning as they were having breakfast, Paul again turned up.

"If you're going shopping, I could show you the best shops," he cheerfully told them.

"If we're going we'd better go now," Annie said, "Before it gets too hot and crowded."

"Fine by me," Sally agreed, "What do we need?"

Lets just look around, we shall find we need it when we see it," said Annie frivolously, she didn't normally enjoy shopping, as did her friend Rose, but here—she decided to relax and, yes, a brightly coloured Kaftan would be most suitable for the evenings and the coast.

They found a covered market and decided on some batiks to take home for presents. The stall holders overwhelmed them; they were not used to such enthusiastic persistence. Paul materialized out of nowhere, cleared a way for them and helped them to find a way out.

"A pity," said Sally regretfully, "There was so much there and we could have bargained."

"There are quieter shops," said Paul.

"But they're so touristy," she replied.

"We are tourists," Annie pointed out.

They followed Paul to his idea of where they should go and Annie's eyes were caught by a beautiful bright Kaftan which was just what she had in mind. She went into the shop confident that Sally was behind her. It was not until she was holding it up against herself that she turned for approval and saw that her daughter was not longer with her, Paul, too had disappeared.

"Don't sell it to anyone else," she said to the salesgirl, "I'm coming back for it."

As she was leaving the shop Sally reappeared. "You must come Mum," she said excitedly, "We can come back here."

"We certainly shall," agreed Annie reluctantly leaving the splendid array of garments. "What's happened?" she added anxiously.

"I've found a wonderful trip, we must go, they've only two places left, they need some money so you must come, it goes tomorrow."

"A trip to where?"

"Lake Turkana, have you ever been there?" She didn't wait for an answer, "Please hurry, it's the Jade Sea and we must see it. It's a truck and camping, they provide everything—well—nearly everything, it sounds wonderful, we must go!"

Annie had felt all along that Sally would be looking for something a little more rugged than an excellent Nairobi hotel and friends wanting to fete them. At the same time she felt that Sally's project of research into her family roots did not take them into remote northern parts of the country. Annie could let her go on her own and agreed when Sally said, "I wish Bob was here," when she saw her Mother's reluctance.

"Okay, show me," was all Annie said. "No," she added, "I've never seen the Jade Sea, I should very much like to."

The office was two doors away, it was small but the window showed magnificent pictures of African scenery and animals.

"One camping spot is at Sambura, the wildlife game lodge there, just look at what we might see."

The young man in the office smiled hopefully at Sally's enthusiasm. "I'm John," he said. "It's my safari and I go with it, I got back yesterday and we're off again tomorrow. Would you like to pay in full?" he added, looking at Annie. "Its not all students," he continued, "there are often some older people, who don't mind roughing it a bit and who are keen to see something of the country."

Annie thought he looked tired, she started to count out the money, it did seem extraordinarily reasonable, she hesitated. "What do we need?" she asked.

"Here's a list of all you need, we supply the rest, tents, mattresses, benches, food, I've a reasonably good cook—you'll enjoy it."

"I'm sure," agreed Annie as she paid up. In any case, she thought it'll be something to boast about back home, the school African project wasn't only about the best hotels and the tourist trade.

"Good," said John, "Be here at seven, there are twenty places, it's full up now, mostly students. See you then."

Weren't we lucky?" Sally was exultant.

"I suppose so," Annie answered, "But I do assure you that if you are searching for your roots and our past this trip is entirely wasted. None of us ever ventured into what was then uncharted country. Nowadays its part of the tourist trade. I am recent history."

Sally was undaunted, "Let's look at the list," was all she said.

"Sensible clothes, sleeping bags," Sally read. "Did you bring a sleeping bag? Oh! It doesn't matter, you can hire one."

"I shall buy one thank you, and I'm going back to buy that Kaftan."

"I might get one too, could be useful on the coast."

"Not much use on a truck I'll admit, and we should just about have enough time for the coast trip."

"You promised."

"Let me remind you that a rough riding truck wasn't in our itinerary."

But Sally wasn't listening, she had spotted a book shop and was already halfway to it. Annie followed, Sally had made a beeline for books and booklets on the various attractions, the wildlife parks, hotels on the coast and the entertainments of the town.

Annie sighed, "Two weeks," she reminded Sally.

Even Sally was reluctant and fretful when their alarm went off in the early morning, she turned over with a grunt when Annie shook her and unkindly pointed out that it was her idea and that the truck left at 7.00. They made it in time and joined the other members of the party at the appointed place. John was waiting for them by the truck.

"I bought it second-hand," he said proudly.

"It looks like it," muttered Annie, only Sally heard. She looked reproachfully at her Mother, "It looks absolutely fine to me." They boarded the vehicle, everyone eyeing each other warily. There were two older people—an obvious couple, a mixed bunch of students and two women of about Annie's age. One was hung about with expensive equipment and dressed in the sort of clothes that are advertised for Safaris, 'perhaps an American' Annie thought. The other was plump and fair, who later turned out to be Danish. There was also a couple who might be honeymooning. "I wouldn't choose this for my honeymoon," said Sally.

"It could be for they might have been a couple for years."

"Yes, I see and this is the holiday of a lifetime?"

They were off, John drove with his two men beside him, one, he had explained, was the cook and the other a good driver but both helped in general ways as did all the passengers when they set up camp. Everyone was also expected to collect wood when they stopped, this was for the evening fire and cooking.

They left the town and were soon on their way to the 'remote parts' and an adventure that Sally's mind was set on. She constantly pointed out various things she thought Annie shouldn't miss. Annie was amused as she was perfectly familiar with the appearance of Mount Kenya with its twin peaks. She was worried, "I forgot to leave a message for the Kimothos."

"Don't be so fidgety, enjoy the ride and anyway I told them at the desk that we'd be away for a few days. Paul was there, he'd be around, I think he wants to meet up with Brenda again.

But Paul was not in Nairobi for, after a somewhat bumpy and dusty drive, they arrived at the Samburu campsite, he was waiting for them ready to help them set up camp.

"I don't encourage my clients to bring their own servants," John complained, "but in this case he seems to have arranged his own transport and he is being a help to Mbugwa, my cook, as well as you, and Mbugwa does seem a bit out of sorts."

"He isn't a servant, he's a young friend," said Annie indignantly. "He was in England and I just happened to do him a good turn."

"A very good turn," put in Sally, "She got him out of prison."

John was startled, "Out of prison, but why and how?"

"It's a long story, not worth telling."

Sally clicked her tongue, "That's Mother," she said. "She'll never tell you the truth; she does that sort of thing."

"Oh! Shut up Sally," said Annie, and to John she replied, "I am a teacher, only things happen to me!"

John was called away by Mbugwa. As he went he said, "I'm going to hear that story sometime."

"And I shall hear yours," replied Annie. She was sure that there was one.

It was a wonderful warm evening, wood had been collected during the day and Mbugwa and Daniel, the other driver, helped by Paul, made a magnificent meal. "It seems magnificent anyway," said Sally, who was now making friends with some of the students. "It may not be five star," agreed Harry, a lanky student from Manchester, "but out here in this setting who would want better." All agreed with him. John blossomed with their praise and told them a little of the place.

"There's an airstrip and a swimming pool here now and so much wildlife, the river is the Uaso Nyiro river, there are crocs there, the swimming pool is safe, don't try the river. We'll do the park tomorrow and have another night here."

Everyone was tired; the two people tents were not exactly luxurious but no-one grumbled. The elderly couple, Victor and Betty Richardson, were not happy, Victor said he didn't feel well and Betty had slept badly. No-one took much notice, they decided to stay at the camp for the day and not to join the day trip, they would use the lodge facilities, including meals. John was happy to leave them. He drove the rest of the party into the park, Paul and the other two Kenyans stayed to mind the camp.

Sally began to get dreamy as they travelled through the park. "It would be far more romantic with camels," she sighed.

"I don't find romance in camels," replied Annie, "they make funny noises and spit."

"They have wonderful eyelashes."

Annie was impatient and once more pointed out that this expedition had not been her choice, she had a job to do and only two weeks on holiday here—also that her history did not lie in this part of the country.

Sally was hurt and moved her seat to join the student group. She returned however, still cheerful and happy.

"Isn't it wonderful, aren't you glad we came."

Annie assured her that she wouldn't have missed it for worlds especially when they saw elephants for at that point she really meant it.

Back at the camp in the evening Annie had gone to the lodge for a drink and to watch the birds. It was here that she first felt uneasy. Was someone watching her—if so why?

John joined her, "I like my clients to be happy. Is something worrying you?"

"There seems to be someone watching me, there's a shifty looking bloke with your two and Paul isn't there. It may be my imagination but yes, it makes me uneasy."

"I've seen him and I'll see he goes. Is there any reason why you are being followed? This teacher business, is it a blind, a mask for your real activities?"

"Good God! No! I really am a teacher, it's just as I said before that things happen round me." She told him the full story of Paul's troubles and how she had tried not to get involved.

He was sympathetic and told her some of his own history. He had set up on his own, "Mainly," he said, "for students. A rough and ready safari that I thought they'd enjoy and learn something. I want it to be a success if possible—I don't want trouble."

The Richardsons then joined them. Victor was still complaining about pains.

"We've asked if they have room here and they have, we've decided to stay and not continue with you." They didn't wait for an answer but walked purposefully away.

Annie and John looked at each other, "they might have said, "Do you mind," said Annie.

"Or a thank you would have done," replied John. He brightened, "but they have paid and didn't ask for their money back."

They both laughed and went back to their talk of the Safari. Before long they were again interrupted, this time by a tall military looking man in his fifties.

"Is it true that someone has opted out and that you might have a vacancy," he said in a parade ground voice, "I wish to visit Turkana."

"Why not?" replied John, "Yes, two have fallen out, are you on your own, if so you'd have a tent to yourself."

"Gordon Jackson," said the man, "Thank you, I'll pay you now, is it extra for the whole tent?" He smiled and said in a much quieter voice, "Is this lady on the outing?"

When he had gone Annie said, "He'll need a whole tent, he's a big man but I hope he quietens down a bit."

"You'll have no troubles now; I think he's an ex-policeman."

Annie agreed although she was not quite happy about the way he had eyed her.

"But I shall still speak to that man; I didn't like the look of him either."

The stranger, an ugly shifty-looking character, was in the camp when they returned for supper. John did this trip regularly and the men knew their routine, were used to it and were happy with it, they were not happy now. Supper was not ready and there was a feeling of unrest in the camp. John summed up the situation and, rather roughly, spoke to the man in Swahili telling him, as Sally put it, 'to f . . . off'. He slunk away, not long after this Paul reappeared and supper was served.

"What was that all about?" Sally asked later as they 'sardined' (Sally's words) into their tent.

"I've no idea except that the Richardsons are leaving us and we have picked up a large man who might be a police officer."

Sally wasn't listening to the answer, "Turkana tomorrow," was all she said as they settled down to sleep, Annie felt extra comfortable as she seemed to have gained an extra mattress.

Their sleep was disturbed in the night, there was shouting and noises of a struggle. Annie sat up and after a while, as the racket increased, Sally too woke up. "What the . . ." There were screams and they heard John's voice.

They peered out of their tent, others were shining torches and grumbling, some were flinging on garments.

The screaming stopped, it sounded more like sobbing now, John's voice came through the darkness. "It's okay," he said. "Go back to bed—a local affair."

The camp quietened down, but Annie sat up outside the tent. I have to know she told herself, perhaps that's my trouble, I'm too nosey. She took her blow-up cushion and sat by the dying embers of the fire. John joined her later, sitting cross-legged on the ground.

"That man reappeared, he tried to bribe Mbugwa, when Mbugwa refused and told him where to go. He picked up a red hot stick from the fire and attacked him."

"Is he badly hurt?"

"Well, he's not happy and has some nasty burns. Some local family and friends joined in and they have taken him somewhere. The troublemaker made his escape."

"What was it about?"

"You, I think. Are you sure you're not onto something? A government spy perhaps?"

"Good God! Whatever next? Are you joking? It can have nothing whatsoever to do with me." Annie was indignant, "how could it?"

The bribe was to do with restricting your activities in some way. The 'some way' meant no good to you, a broken arm or leg—something simple like that."

"Oh! Thanks very much for telling me."

"Don't worry, you will have a guard the rest of the way, or so I'm told. Is it okay if I employ your Paul instead of Mbugwa, or until we return from Turkana?"

"He'll be glad I'm sure, its no problem to me," replied Annie, now totally puzzled.

"I don't understand it, I've done nothing, I'm on holiday."

John sighed and muttered something which sounded like 'the lady doth protest too much'.

Annie let it go and retired to the tent for the rest of the night, Sally was already asleep again. "Oh to be young," said Annie to herself as she struggled into her sleeping bag once more.

Next morning Paul had already blown up the fire for tea, there was a hurried breakfast before breaking camp and boarding the truck once more. John kept to his story of a local feud to account for the night disturbance. Nobody seemed to be very bothered, a change of cook made very little difference and Paul had been about most of the time anyway.

"Would he come to me permanently do you think," John asked Annie. "He's a good cook, he says he can drive and he's intelligent, what do you think?"

"I think his brother wants him to be a teacher and go to College, but it's definitely not my affair."

They were joined by Gordon Jackson in the truck, Sally was talking to the other students, Annie was in her usual seat and the empty place beside her was taken by Gordon. He looked pleased and well satisfied.

Annie wondered if this was her guard, had it been fixed all along and if so why?

CHAPTER 7

AS THEY TRAVELLED NORTH THE road became progressively worse, the vegetation was now sparse and the stony road, if it was a road, extremely dusty. "It's a desert," exclaimed one of the students. As they descended across the lava flows they caught their first glimpse of the lake, rightly called the Jade Sea. It really was that wonderful colour and the sight of it made everyone gasp, the contrast between the shimmering water and the terrain where they stopped for a moment was immense. They had stopped to lower the hood of the truck, some wanted to take photos, some just to look. "It's like a mirage," said another student.

"This rugged desert look must be good enough even for you," Annie said to Sally as she joined her daughter by the side of the truck.

"I knew it would be wonderful, aren't you glad we came?" replied Sally.

They drove down to the lake and set up camp under a clump of dry looking trees. The party then broke up into various groups. Annie and Sally were quickly into swimming costumes with only one thought in their minds of 'let's get in it'. Barbara and the Danish girl went away to find suitable photographic subjects. Gordon and two other students prepared to follow Annie. John shouted after them to mind the crocs before setting out with the remaining students to collect more wood for the evening fire, leaving Paul and Daniel behind in charge of the camp with orders to buy fish if anyone came selling it.

It was a strange hard beach unlike anything the bathers had come across before. They saw no crocodiles; they splashed happily in the wonderful water and then cool, clean and refreshed they returned to camp where Gordon and Paul organized tea on an emergency cooking stove. This was to Annie's delight, as tea was not on the timetable.

Later that evening, after a delicious fish supper and as they relaxed, satisfied and happy round the camp fire, John asked if they minded if they changed the itinerary slightly so that they return this time to Samburu.

"I usually do a round trip but I want to pick something up that I left behind."

No-one objected, Gordon even giving a sigh of relief as he, too, had left quite a bit behind. "I hadn't realized then that you didn't normally return that way," he said.

"We stay another night here," John went on, "Tomorrow we'll visit the El Molo village tribe and also anywhere else you particularly want to see." We'll stop at Nakuru and I promise you Lake Baringo to see the hippos.

Everyone was happy with that arrangement, they'd seen the lake, some had been in it, they'd seen the Rift Valley and the surrounding countryside—that was all they asked—and hippos-well-good.

John followed Annie back to her tent when they all finally retired.

"I didn't tell anyone that the racket and brawl back at Samburu concerned one of my men. I didn't want to worry everyone, I make light of it, said it was a local matter. What I want to do is to see if he's okay, if he is we'll take him back with us."

"Wise move," agreed Annie.

They were tired and dusty when they arrived back at Samburu; the road had been particularly bad, they'd had a puncture and run out of food. "All part of an exciting trip," someone remarked.

"We saw the wallowing hippos," said Gordon.

"And we did find someone with bananas," put in Sally cheerfully.

All agreed that it had been worth it.

At Samburu it was obvious by the large police presence that something was wrong at the lodge.

"Let's set up camp," John said, "before you all head for the pool. While you do that I'll go and find out what's going on. With any luck we're not involved."

Before he had started two policemen were seen coming towards them.

The more senior of the two men enquired where they had been. No-one answered, they all felt it was up to John to speak for them, in any case some were not sure where they had been, it was John's business.

"What's going on?" he asked.

"A murdered man Sir, found in the garden here, not a local man and no-one seems to know him."

"They never do," said John, "If I know Kenya, and I do, I've lived here all my life, no-one will have seen him before," he sighed, "When was this?"

"The night before last Sir."

"You were soon on the job."

"We had a tip-off, Sir."

"How was he killed?"

"Shot, and no-one heard the shot either."

"That's not surprising," said John, "He could have been killed elsewhere and the body brought here," he thought for a moment. "I'm sorry I can't be of much help but . . . if there is anything I can do let me know," he prepared to turn away but the officer said, "Would you mind taking a look at the body, Sir, it might help us in some way?"

"I don't see how," John replied "But I'll come willingly."

He shook his head as he viewed the body of their shifty follower. "Sorry," he said, He must have come from some different tribe or just someone from a town perhaps. Not much help from us I'm afraid."

He returned to the camp and sought Annie.

"Can we talk?" he asked her. She was sitting outside her tent and looked up questioningly, startled by his anxious tone.

"What happened?" she asked.

"There's been a murder," he replied. "I shan't tell you who the victim is, perhaps you can guess."

"Not Mbugwa, I hope?" Annie asked.

"No, the other one, we shall have no follower on the way home. Revenge I expect. Would you recognize him if asked," he enquired.

"Certainly not," answered Annie.

"Oh! Good, I don't want to be held up here. We only came to pick up Mbugwa. What shall I do?"

"I suggest we find Mbugwa first, where is he likely to be?" said Annie in a practiced way.

"Daniel came to me with an odd story," said John ignoring Annie's question. "Apparently this man came to them with money as payment for 'putting you out of business'. You tell me you're a teacher, are you working for someone, is something going on?"

"I've no idea, I do assure you . . ."

"This large police presence is suspicious for a start; if there's anything I should know about please tell me, I've a business to run."

"Find Mbugwa, Paul can go back the way he came, we brought two, we return with two. Was it a head wound or a burn. Buy him a new hat," finished Annie.

"There's no sign of Mbugwa."

He was wrong there, Mbugwa stepped out of the shadows, he was standing in the shade of trees behind them.

"A new hat?" he asked hopefully.

They looked at him. "I tell you what," said Annie, "Sally bought one to take home to Bob her boyfriend, it's in the tent." She rose and went into the tent returning with the hat. "I'll buy another one for Bob."

Mbugwa took the hat and put it one. "Very fine hat," he said.

"Early tomorrow," said John.

"We'll call him Luke," proposed Annie. "No-one will notice."

"What about that Gordon Jackson, or is he too busy looking at you?" enquired John. "Can you fix him too?"

Annie looked daggers at him, but made no reply.

Gordon appeared and saying 'excuse me' to John asked Annie if she would like to come over to the lodge for a drink, "You too John, if you like, there are several of us there."

John gave Annie a long look but replied that he had things to do. He departed after giving Annie another knowing look. Annie, annoyed, accepted Gordon's offer and went with him to the bar.

"There's talk—that is I overhead Sally say that you were going to the coast and I wondered if I could be of any help?" Gordon asked when they were settled with their drinks.

"In what way?" Annie wanted to know.

"I have to go to Mombasa on business; I have a car big enough for us all including your man and any luggage."

Annie replied that she must consult Sally, she made no comment about Paul, she was tired of telling people that he was a friend and not a servant. At the moment, too, she didn't wish to draw attention to the working team. She could see Sally at the far end of the room and when Gordon went to refill their glasses Annie went over to her and told her of his suggestion.

"But Mum, you said we could go by train," Sally expostulated. "Or we thought we could hire a car and return by train."

One of her friends, listening unashamedly, said, "But you'd save money, or have you plenty," she added enviously.

"There is that," agreed Sally. "He could drive us there; shall we be able to get rid of him?"

"He said he had business there."

"Oh! Good. In that case he wouldn't be trailing us."

"Certainly not, its different here, space is limited and it would save the shillings. Its not a bad idea if you don't mind and we can take Paul."

"He'll be driving so we can enjoy the scenery, you decide Ma, but yes, it's okay by me."

Gordon spotted them and came over with the drinks. "Can I get you anything Sally?" he asked.

"No thank you, I'm off to bed."

Annie looking round saw many hopeful faces and empty glasses. "I'm going too," she told Gordon. "We've decided to accept your very generous offer of a lift to Mombasa," she added and left him to it.

John was in the camp when they arrived. Annie smiled at him. "I should like to correct you on two points," she said, "One, I do not 'fix' it for people and two, that man is not a permanent attachment."

John looked confused but Sally laughed as she crawled into the inadequate tent.

"Come off it Ma," she giggled, "We can't do anything without you picking up a man."

"For God's sake," said Annie, following her into the tent and zipping up the entrance.

John made sure it was an early start next morning while Annie satisfied herself that Paul knew what was happening and had enough money for whatever means he used to return to Nairobi. "We'll see you there," she told him.

John had the bright idea of pushing the truck until they were out of sight of the lodge, "So as not to disturb anyone," he explained. No-one was at all suspicious and all gave a hand feeling virtuous and thoughtful. When on the road they all boarded and were on their way.

Annie was very casual when Gordon started to show an interest as to which man was which. Paul had helped with the pushing and then discreetly withdrawn.

"Which is your man?" Gordon asked, "Wasn't that him?"

"Oh! He has friends here, he's going back with them later. They all share duties, works out very well don't you think, it doesn't matter who does what and they're all wearing the same hat."

He laughed and Annie asked about his timetable. She could see no reason for her feeling of guilt, was she doing what John had called 'fixing him'? We've done no wrong, she told herself, probably her shifty follower had been nosing about near the Samburu tribe, too

close, perhaps, for their comfort. She was sure that Mbugwa was not
the murderer. He was the injured party, and didn't want to be involved
in 'removing' her. Why, she thought, would anyone want to 'remove'
me? What am I supposed to be doing? She could think of no answer
so with a clear conscience she listened to Gordon's plans for the coastal
trip.

"Tomorrow then?" he was saying, "You'd like to go
tomorrow."

"No, the day after please, if that's okay with you."

"Perfectly, so I'll collect you from 'The Norfolk' shall I? At
what time?"

"Not the hotel, we have neglected our friends and must make
contact with them. They asked us to stay you see. I think they live at
Karen."

"I have friends there too, no problem."

When they arrived at the dropping off point in Nairobi there
was a group of people waiting there for them. "Its Dr Kimotho," said
Annie, "He must have second sight or how did he know?"

"It's the bush telegraph," laughed Gordon, "Oh! Good, I know
Dr Kimotho slightly," he paused, "But not the man with him."

Annie looked again, there was no mistaking that lean figure—it
was Neil.

CHAPTER 8

WHEN THE TRUCK STOPPED THERE was a silence. It was if someone had written *The End*. Then there was a burst of sound and the descent from the truck was noisily emotional. Everyone was doing something, jumping down from the truck, collecting luggage, hugging, kissing, shaking hands and everyone assuring everyone else how they would all meet again. There were 'thankyous' to John and the crew, telling them and each other how wonderful it had been.

Gordon helped Annie down from the truck with the air of someone entitled to do so, he collected her luggage and carried it in a possessive way. Annie didn't look at Neil, she didn't have to, she could feel his antagonism.

They shook hands with Dr Kimotho who said. "Oh! You know Gordon do you, a good friend." Gordon bowed slightly acknowledging the compliment, to Annie he said, "I'll see you tomorrow then, to fix details for the trip." He departed, Neil looked daggers after him.

Sally then joined them having waved 'goodbye' to her new friends. "Hello Neil," she said in a friendly way.

"Do you know the Superintendent?" asked Dr Kimotho, who was ready with his introductions, he sounded surprised.

"We have met," admitted Annie.

"I expect," said Dr Kimotho, "That it was on one of your cases."

"That was probably it," she replied thinking, "what's the use, everyone is sure that I'm a private detective."

"Superintendent LaCoste is staying with us over Christmas. He is a guest of our police, you will perhaps meet the Chief of Police who too is joining us for our Christmas feast tomorrow. The Superintendent has been asked over so that they can share ideas on this terrible trafficking of women and children, to our mutual benefit they believe," Dr Kimotho explained. "The discussion," he added, "not the trafficking."

Sally interrupted, "Is it really Christmas Day tomorrow, it doesn't feel like it."

"Is your friend also joining us?" Neil asked Dr Kimotho.

"I haven't asked him," he replied. Neil was puzzled, but he said, "See you tomorrow Mrs Butcher."

"He's driving us to the coast the day after," Annie told him cheerfully. "Sally and Paul are both coming," she added with a smile.

"Good," Neil said, "Then you will have company and protection." To Dr Kimotho he said, "I shall enjoy renewing my acquaintance with Mrs Butcher and her daughter."

"Please do call me Annie," she said, falling into the spirit of the thing and this unexpected meeting.

Dr Kimotho broke into this exchange, so you will be staying with us for two nights, Gordon can pick you up from here, we have already collected your things from the hotel."

Annie thanked him, she wasn't happy about his organisation but accepted it, she looked at Sally who shrugged.

"We've no alternative," said Annie to her later, "They are being so kind, but we'll assert ourselves when we are washed and fed for if it's Christmas tomorrow they'll shower us with presents, we'll depart firmly for the shops later as we haven't much to give in return." Neil joined them in being firm, he had hired a car and offered to take them to the shops as he, too, had some things to buy.

They were tired when they returned but had enough gifts to add to the general present-giving next day. Annie was embarrassed by being honoured and endlessly thanked for something she felt she didn't deserve but Sally was lapping it up. Christmas Day was, as far as she was concerned, all that it should be, she had slept well and was full of food, Neil had given her a most expensive bracelet so that when Gordon arrived on Boxing Day to pick them up she was ready for anything. She wondered what Neil had given her Mother but decided not to ask.

Gordon's car was a big one, he and Dr Kimotho, (now Douglas for they were now on first name terms) settled into it assuring them how much they would enjoy the trip. Neil stood by, disapproval written all over him. Sally in a happy mood kissed him 'Goodbye' but Annie waved cheerfully. They picked Paul up at the Norfolk.

They were soon out of the town and on the coast road. Gordon drove steadily, he wanted to make sure his passengers saw everything, they were in his care, he talked most of the time making sure that they didn't miss any outcrop, tree or animal that was worthy of their notice. Paul sometimes added a few comments of his own. It was great, thought Annie, that these two had her interests at heart and although Sally was happily asking questions and obediently responding to all the observations and demands for her attention. Annie, glad of Sally's enthusiasm, quietly dozed. They pulled into a driveway for refreshments supplied by Gordon and were quietly enjoying these when they were jolted into unpleasant reality by events around them. A car had pulled up in the road just ahead of them, why in that particular place they were never quite sure—perhaps another car parked in a lay by and its occupants peacefully picnicking was reassuring, but then a larger vehicle came too fast, pulled over as a truck was coming in the other direction, it braked, but not soon enough, hit the smaller parked car pushing it onto its side and into the bushes. The big car seemed not to be damaged as it reversed and drove off fast. There was much noise, shouting, children crying, engines revving and metal scraping, picnic peace was over. The oncoming truck had not stopped. Gordon and Paul rushed to the tilted car and helped to release the unhappy occupants. The driver, a woman, was clinging to Gordon.

"It was this big car, my children wanted to stop—they thought they saw some animals in the bushes, I was only stopping for a minute, I'm sure it had been following us and much too closely, it was going much too fast—my daughter has hurt her arm—I'm sure I've got a black eye, the car's a write-off, its only hired, what will they say, we're only here for another week," she was getting hysterical.

Another car drew up and a large party of helpful Africans got out and joined the gathering around the battered car.

Sally looked at Annie, "What shall we do?" she asked. Gordon seemed to be fully occupied, another car was drawing up, "He'll be busy for some time," she continued. "I think I'll go down to those buildings, it looks as if there's a sizeable bungalow down there."

"Good idea," agreed Annie, "I think I'll just stay here and await developments."

Sally disappeared down the track.

Annie found an unopened thermos full of tea, she sat in the car, she didn't feel obliged to join the group, there were plenty of people there and more cars were stopping.

Sally returned triumphant, "There's quite a community down there and a school, someone remembers you . . . well—vaguely, were you Eleanor Aldridge's daughter, is that you?"

Annie admitted to it, "What's on down there?" she asked.

"It's a bit of a party for something or other, they're having lunch, we've been invited, do come down, it'll be fun," she paused, "I'd better tell Paul."

"And I'd better tell Gordon, but they'll know where we are."

At that moment Gordon came over, he was apologetic, "They're very upset and I've said I'll drive them back to Nairobi. I wouldn't have promised only the couple in that blue car have offered to take you onto the coast, I'll join you down there tomorrow."

He was inclined to be huffy when Annie suggested that the distressed mother was clingy.

"Not at all," he said, "She's naturally in a bad state, her husband is still in Nairobi."

"Isn't there a bus on this road?" asked Annie.

"Not the sort you would wish to go on," was his reply.

Annie could think of plenty of retorts to this but she refrained.

"It's okay anyway," put in Sally, "We've an invitation down there in that bungalow, some old friends of my mothers."

Annie felt that this was not entirely truthful but she only said, "We'll be fine Gordon, honestly, do please help those people and tell the people in the blue car that we have no need of a lift."

Gordon collected his charges and drove off after Sally had removed the luggage from his car. Paul refused to accompany him, he would not leave Annie in spite of Gordon's pressing requests.

"I'll carry the luggage down there for you and there's bound to be someone there I know." Paul reassured them. Annie was glad of his help but she was more worried about arriving at a lunch party with so much luggage, for Sally hadn't restricted herself in any way. "You never know who we might meet," she had said.

It was not only luggage that was worrying Annie for their immediate future seemed a little unsettled, she was sure something would turn up, perhaps they were not far from a railway station and could get a lift there, they could always come back to the road and hitch a lift (or could they?) perhaps it wouldn't be wise. Meanwhile there were these old for new(?) friends to meet.

Sally had already told of the happenings on the road and of their present predicament but Annie now added further explanations to account for their luggage now piled up on the veranda. Everyone was sympathetic, varying types of help were suggested but Mary's idea that they all tucked into the refreshments seemed the best. Mary was the owner of the bungalow and their unexpected hostess,

"We're having a bit of a party for Clare's birthday," Mary told them.

"Clare?" asked Annie, looking round her.

"I'm Clare, I'm a teacher at the school, this is my friend and fellow teacher Hilary," both girls came forward. They had been looking rather hungrily at the laden table which also held a most appetizing looking birthday cake.

Both girls were in their early twenties, Hilary was small, wiry and dark whereas Clare was built on much sturdier lines and was a redhead.

Hilary said, "We're graduate VSOs, we were at Uni together in Birmingham but a Maths degree and an English degree are not what are really needed here." They looked at each other and laughed.

"But we've got a house," said Clare.

"Of sorts," added Hilary, "you must come and see it."

"We'd love to," replied Annie.

They all moved towards the food, encouraged by Mary, the ice was soon broken but everyone had been so friendly that Annie thought there had been little ice anyway.

"We're a bit full up in the bungalow at the moment," said Mary. "There is the veranda . . ."

"No," said Clare, "We've plenty of room, it's a bit basic and it's only a bunk bed and we haven't any extra bed linen but . . ."

"Great," said Sally, "we've got sleeping bags, I wondered when we were going to use them."

"Come over and see," urged Hilary.

"We'll do just that," agreed Annie.

The party broke up in the early afternoon, all were going in different directions.

"We've got the school car and it isn't far," Clare said as they approached an old jalopy of very doubtful make. "We can ask Tom, Tom Rato that is, our head master, if we can borrow it and take you to the coast, he might agree."

Annie and Sally climbed in the back, Annie was doubtful if it would make it to the school, let alone the coast, but as Clare and Hilary seemed so pleased with it she did not mention her doubts. They did arrive at the school.

"We've forgotten the luggage," exclaimed Sally. But no! There it was hung round an old bicycle which Paul had managed to borrow and there he was himself beside the headmaster at the door of the school, "Your friend brought it over," said Tom Rato stepping forward to shake hands.

"What I like about Africa, or this bit of it anyway," Sally said to her Mother as they followed the others into the school, "Is the way everyone knows what you are going to do before you do it."

"It's known as the bush telegraph, didn't you know," replied her Mother, but her mind was on the school—this was just what the 'George Pound' wanted, here was a real African school, she could hardly wait to put her suggestion to Tom Rato.

She didn't waste any time for as he showed them round she asked, "Would you be willing to 'twin' with an English school? The school where I teach is a little bigger than this," she crossed her fingers at this gross understatement. "My head teacher asked me to look out for a suitable establishment."

Mr Rato was delighted at the idea. He clapped his hands and almost jumped up and down with pleasure, "Tell me more, what would happen? Should I have to go to England, what is your school like, is it better than this?"

Annie thought they might be there for a week if she told him of the many differences, perhaps she could get Clare and Hilary to tell him more about schooling in Britain, but they, taking advantage of his obvious good mood, were already asking for the loan of the precious school car in order to drive Annie and Sally to the coast, "for they HAVE to be there tomorrow."

They would not be missed they assured him for tomorrow was a half holiday and the day after that was Saturday and a non-school day. The students they had left in charge of their classes would oversee their work and he was there anyway. He had agreed almost without considering the matter, his mind being on the greater subject—the wonderful twinning scheme.

Annie was not happy about leaving classes but, as they went round the school, saw that older children, not exactly students, had been left in charge while Clare and Hilary went to the birthday party. This was hardly a practice that would have been allowed at the 'George Pound'. She said nothing, however, on that subject but saved her breath for a few words in each class, telling them about her own school. She found them bright and eager to learn, they were all Kenyans, there were no European faces. Their work was neat and tidy, it was obvious that

Mr Rato did not believe in distracting activities. This was exactly the school she was looking for.

"We'll be in touch," she told Tom as they all left to view the young teachers' bungalow. Paul was to be the honoured guest, he was going home with Tom Rato.

They slept well after a trip to the main road to see if anything had happened up there, but all had been cleared away.

"We shall have to wait to see Gordon again before we know the outcome," Annie said.

"If he comes back," replied Sally doubtfully.

They were all off next morning, Paul did not accompany them.

"I'll hitch," he said, "and then if I see you stuck on the road, I'll be able to give you a push." Clare and Hilary were indignant but Paul only laughed, "I'll see you there," he told them.

Annie and Sally were booked in at a hotel on the beach in Mombasa, but the two teachers had been lent a cottage some distance from the town, they had the key to this. They all said their goodbyes but were sure of meeting again if the twinning took place. Annie and Sally were returning to Nairobi by train.

CHAPTER 9

THEY WENT TO THE DESK of the hotel after waving the old car off. "We can always hire a car if we want to go anywhere," Annie said, Sally looked astonished.

"This is where I want to be," she declared, "where else would we want to be, I certainly don't want to go anywhere."

Annie laughed, "Its okay by me and when its time to go we can get a taxi to the station."

Paul was there to greet them, they wandered how he had managed to be there before them, they endlessly marvelled at his ability to be in several places at once. Annie began to understand his absolute misery when confined in Youth Custody.

"I hitched a lift," he now told them. "Didn't you notice that several cars passed you?" They had noticed but had looked the other way, preferring to believe or hope that others on the road thought they travelled that way from choice.

Paul now looked grave, "I'm worried, do you remember that large car, the one that caused the accident?"

They did remember, "A Toyota wasn't it?" asked Sally.

"It's in the car park here, I just checked on it, it's the same one I'm sure. I'm also sure it wasn't following them, for the early part of the journey it was following us."

Sally turned on him, "Don't spoil everything Paul, you're jittery, imagining things, why should anyone bother to follow us. You need a holiday, a few days here will do you a world of good.

"I'm sure we're okay," added Annie. "Have they fixed you up all right?"

"I'll see where you are before I decide where to sleep." He was obviously not happy, "That Gordon was supposed to be looking after you. Dr. Kimotho especially asked him, it's because of this corruption business."

They didn't listen to him, they were too interested in the evening entertainment. It was African night at the hotel, a receptionist was enthusiastic.

"Lots of dancing, lots of good food and drink, music, a happy night, you must be there." They promised to be there, collected the key to their chalet and set off along the beach to view it. It was a double chalet under palm trees and overlooking the sea. "Wonderful," said Sally enthused. "Just what I imagined." They settled in and took a walk along the beach, marvelling at the sparkling water, they picked up bits of pink coral which Sally said she intended to make into a necklace, "sometime or other."

Paul assured them that he was going to sleep in the open air and in view of their hut.

"Shall you come to the dance?" Annie asked him.

"Just try to keep me away," he replied as he wandered off.

After a quick dip Annie and Sally dressed in their new Kaftans and when the music started strolled over to the main building for the evening's amusement. It was a perfect night and they had every intention of enjoying themselves.

The music was good as was all the food when, later in the evening, it was laid out upon the floor and they all sat cross-legged beside this feast and helped themselves. When this interlude was over, for the band had joined the feast, the music started up again. It was too dark, for the lamps were low, to see very far or with whom one was dancing, Annie could no longer see Sally and she herself was dancing with a young American who frequently referred to her charming English accent. She could tell he was American as his was very pronounced, and young, she thought as his voice suggested, youth. It's too dark for him to see how old I am and fortunately I am not yet creaking at the joints. I wonder, she thought as with her partner she gyrated and bottom rotated around the floor, I wonder if we could do something like this at the George Pound. Some of the younger teachers had joined a class of Belly Dancing. When I get home perhaps I should join this, at least we could discuss the possibility of an African night. I should do more of this before it's too late. Annie was enjoying herself in an uninhibited sort of way and was thankful that Gordon was not there doing his protecting act. Neil now? How would he have reacted? Better not to think of it, music and dancing like this could lead to almost anything.

If he came to the George Pound version which was most unlikely, they would be under the watchful eye of staff, parents and students and, in any case, a dance after the School Gala on a June Midlands evening could hardly be compared to an African Beach Party. Annie banished such thoughts as she enjoyed the present and abandoned herself with enthusiasm to its activities.

At one point her youthful friend had temporarily deserted her, she took the opportunity of slipping away, she was tired and thought of their pleasant chalet under the palm trees and sleep with the sound of gentle waves on the beach. She could not see Sally but Sally would come when she was ready, and where was Paul? Annie hadn't seen him for some time, so with a total disregard for security she left the door open. Paul was bound to be somewhere around and would notice and discourage intruders.

As she dozed she thought of all the dancing 'I really haven't the bottom for it', perhaps back home it would be more seemly to persuade Dudley to organize some Morris dancing. She fell asleep on this soothing thought.

Meanwhile Sally had left the party earlier, her feet hurt and she didn't like the man who had, she felt, been the cause of this discomfort. Not only that she didn't like him, he was heavy and smelly, "If only Bob was here." But Paul should be about, where was he? And was there only one hot, heavy, smelly man? It was dark but she was almost sure that there were two who alternated with her on the dance floor. She began to feel uneasy. As she made for the sea to cool her aching feet she thought 'I think I'll give it a miss—tomorrow is another day.'

She turned towards the chalets but the two men were there, one put a heavy hood over her head and the other tied her arms to her sides, she tried to kick but her long kaftan was then tied with a sack round her ankles. Stifled and helpless she found herself dragged along and pushed into some vehicle, could it be that Toyota?

Paul was about, he had been standing quietly and unseen by the door and he too felt helpless. The two men that followed Sally were big, he had no idea of their intention, keeping in the shadows he followed them to the car park and saw them drive off. He was only temporarily paralyzed, his quick wit returned to him and seeing a nearby motorbike 'borrowed' it, kicked it into action, and followed the Toyota. As there was only one road along the beach he soon saw the tail-lights. The road was rough, dusty and narrow, he was able to follow at a reasonable distance without being obvious, the car turned when a better road led inland, there was a little traffic here so that one motorbike was not conspicuous. The car turned off again after about half a mile. This track looked like a private drive so Paul did not follow but stopped on the better road under a tree. He was worried about petrol, he was sure the bike was giving off noises suggesting imminent immobility. He would walk. He was a good walker and runner, he assured himself, as he set out, that it was unlikely to be very far, nobody with a decent car would want to drive along a track like this for any distance.

Annie awoke, it was quite light, tea is essential and perhaps breakfast, she looked over to the other bed, Sally was not there, had she gone to breakfast already? No, the bed had not been slept in, there were no signs that Sally had ever returned here, she didn't usually leave her things tidily—there was no 'unmade bed' look about the place, neither was she renowned for her early rising, she could have been tempted by the water. These thoughts flitted about in Annie's head. 'It's too early to think,' she told herself, but one thing I must do and that is to get dressed and go over to the hotel and find out what has happened. She decided on a quick dip first, this refreshed her, she wasn't often so muzzy in the morning, but then it wasn't often that she went to an Africa Night in Africa. Perhaps Sally, too, was equally muzzy somewhere, and Paul, where was Paul?

There was no sign of Sally in the hotel, breakfast was in progress in the main restaurant, but there was no sign of her there. Annie went to the reception desk

"I can't find my daughter," she told the young manager who was there.

"Maybe she has gone," he replied vaguely, his thoughts miles away.

"You don't understand, she wouldn't go without me."

He jerked himself into a listening frame of mind, "I'm sorry," he said, "there is trouble in Nairobi."

Annie could not see that this had any bearing on her present troubles. "My daughter," she repeated, "she is missing, should we inform the police?"

"No, no, no police. Police very busy back in Nairobi, political troubles you understand.

"Then who will help me look for her."

"Your friends, your servant perhaps?"

"He is not a servant if you mean Paul Kimani. He's a friend," Annie was indignant and upset by this lack of interest.

"Then your other friend, the one who says he is or was a policeman. He is just going, perhaps you should go with him."

"I'm not going anywhere without my daughter. Not only her but I can't find Paul either?

"Eeee, Ahhhh,"

"No, it's not like that, you don't understand, he helps us, he looks after us . . ." Annie's words trailed off.

"Then perhaps they are with other friends, there are Americans staying here," he managed to imply that anything could happen if Americans were involved.

"Did you say that Gordon, Mr Jackson, has left?"

"No, but he's just about to," said a voice behind her, "and I advise you to do the same. How soon can you be ready? I'm leaving in a few minutes, you can come with me."

"I'm not leaving, I can't find Sally."

He dithered, "I have to go, there are troubles in Nairobi, I can take you to the airport . . . .."

"I said I'm not leaving, in any case we're going back by train."

"If they run, don't be stupid, I'm offering you a safe journey."

Annie was angry, she turned on him. "Go away," she cried at him, "can't you see that I have other things on my mind."

He glared at her, muttered something and turned away.

"He is ex-policeman, he has to go," explained the young manager, Owira. "You will be safe here."

"Safe from what?"

"It is political, it does not affect us."

"It's my daughter I'm worried about."

"Here is the airport bus, the new arrivals, if you will wait awhile I will give you some attention." Owira turned to greet his new guests, there was chatter and bustle. Annie turned to face the newcomers and found herself facing a well known figure. Neil had arrived.

For a moment Annie was speechless, Neil spoke first, "Something is troubling you?"

"Yes, and I was never more pleased to see someone."

He smiled, "Ah, hopeful that, let's sit over there," he indicated a table and chairs a little way from the desk and the collecting holidaymakers. "And, by the way, this is Inspector Musaba of the Nairobi police, he's on a case that seemed to concern you."

Annie looked puzzled, did she endlessly have to explain that whatever it was it was nothing to do with her, she was a teacher on holiday.

"The boy, Kimani, Paul Kimani, he reported that someone was annoying you, on your trip up North," he paused, "and I don't mean lover boy, for the man who runs the safari also reported a worrying incident."

Annie passed over the reference to Gordon and held out her hand to Inspector Musaba.

"How do you do," he said taking her hand, "so now I hear that something has happened," he turned to Neil, "You were wise to suggest that I accompany you. We were at college together," he said to Annie, "I was on a course in England, he was always a very clever man."

A very noisy vehicle was heard approaching, an old motorbike drew up abruptly in a cloud of dust by the entrance, it fell over as its riders climbed off it and, with staggering steps joined the assembly at the reception desk. These riders, dirty, dishevelled, and exhausted, were greeted by Annie's shout. "Sally, Paul, where have you been, I was worried sick," she rushed towards Sally arms outstretched, Sally, too, held out her arms.

"I was kidnapped, it was horrible. I . . . I . . ." she stumbled and before she could reach her Mother, collapsed unconscious in a heap.

Some of the holiday makers were not sure if this was part of an entertainment put on for their benefit so they dutifully clapped. Paul, rising to the occasion bowed but he rushed to Inspector Musaba who put his arms around him and turning to Neil said, "This is my sister's boy I was telling you about, she worries and worries about him, God only knows what he has been up to this time." But Neil was on his knees with Annie beside Sally.

Owira, the perplexed young manager, was out of his depth, and said to Inspector Musaba, "Please will you take your party to my office, it is there behind you, I will have tea and coffee sent to you and deal with your registration later."

Neil lifted Sally and with the Inspector, Paul and Annie went thankfully to this quiet room, Paul fetched more chairs and closed the door behind them.

Sally was recovering, "Put me down," she said to Neil, who, on hearing her voice, was only too willing to do so. He put her in one chair and drew up another for her feet. Tea and coffee arrived, the waiter lingering so as not to miss any excitement that might be going on, or a story that might be suitably exaggerated for the benefit of his fellow workers.

The drinks revived everyone and the story told. It was told in personal instalments, Sally telling her terror, her helplessness and despair because she didn't know what was happening or why. Paul told of his watch and of his consequent following of the Toyota. Inspector Musaba said, "There we are, it's this Toyota again, good lad."

Their listeners were able to piece the story together before deciding on action. Annie's most anxious desire was to get her daughter into a bath and bed before deciding on their next move.

Paul had abandoned the motorbike, "I only borrowed it," and had followed the track to a clearing in the bush. It was a big clearing, big enough to be seen from the air, there were buildings of all sorts within the fence, more of a stockade, Paul thought. He wandered round the outside not daring to go in even if he could find an entrance, there were gates which were securely locked. His eyes were getting used to the gloom and he could see lights in some of the buildings, these varied, some were of wood and some round and built of traditional vegetation. Even if he could get in where would Sally be? He crept on and found that some of the enclosure on the side opposite the gate there was no track and, to Paul's delight, this part of the boundary was made of brushwood. It was wild bush here, it was probably of a temporary nature to allow easy access. It seemed a good place for a reconnoitre, not too close to the lights and dark enough not to be seen. He moved some of the brushwood and was within the enclosure, but the problem was not solved, he still had to find Sally. As well as the buildings there were various vehicles. There was the Toyota, two vans, another battered car and one very good one. Further on there were two trucks. If only he had a light, he felt unhopefully in his pockets and, to his surprise, found a box of matches. Of course—he had pocketed them when he found an outhouse at the hotel, he'd made this place his 'headquarters' but as it had no electricity had found a candle and matches for a light. He now thanked himself for his carelessness and lit a match. It was the same Toyota, he knew the number. He began to feel more confident and this improved again when he realized that he also had his knife. Now he was ready for anything. He continued his inspection of the site, surely Sally must be in one of these huts, if the men had meant to kill her, they could have done it on the beach, they must be holding her for some purpose, a ransom perhaps or a 'keep out of our business' threat. There was a noise from one hut, he crept nearer—it was someone snoring loudly and with an unlikely-to-wake-up sound to it. Whoever it was had not extinguished the light and near to this hut was another smaller hut and beyond that a round falling-down remains of another. Paul looked into this pile first, there was no one in it. He turned his attention to the one next to the snorer, there were definite snuffling noises here. He scratched on the side, not much good, he thought, for I could be a lion. He decided to sing softly and had only started on 'God Save the Queen' when a voice joined him 'Long live our' He had found Sally.

With his knife it was easy to remove the lock, he struck a match, it was easy, too, to cut through her bonds which were only thin ropes, her hood had been removed and replaced with a dirty piece of cloth which served as a gag. Sally swung herself off the camp bed on which she was lying and freed her ankles. She hitched her kaftan up to knee length for convenience. "Bless you!" she said.

He beckoned her to follow him and they went over to the vehicles, "Can you drive?" he asked her. "Of course," she replied, wondering which one he had in mind to steal. He pointed to the smaller truck, he had, on his previous inspection, found that this was the only one not locked and with its keys in it. He only hoped it would start.

"It would be great fun," he whispered, "to set the place on fire." This was not Sally's idea of 'great fun'.

"I suppose," she whispered back, "that a small fire might distract them, it might even hide the noise of the truck's engine. So, okay if you must, just that one small broken down grass hut. Is anyone in it?"

"No, it's empty except for a few old boxes."

"Go on then, have your fun." Paul took out his matches and lit the driest looking bit of thatch, it was smouldering slowly when they reached the truck.

"I'll drive it though the brushwood barrier and onto the track, you can take it from there. I haven't got a driving licence." Sally thought that this was the least of their troubles but agreed to his arrangement. The engine of the truck started immediately and Paul drove fast at the brushwood barrier, through the bush and onto the track. They could now see some satisfactory flames behind them.

"I'm still not sure it was the right thing to do," said Sally as she took over the driving and went as fast as the truck would go over the rough ground. Paul explained about the motor-bike and it was still where he left it when they reached the made-up road. Sally stopped the truck and they loaded the bike into the back. It was at this point that they heard the first explosion. "Someone is having a firework display." suggested Paul as they looked back the way they had come.

"What did you say was in those boxes?" enquired Sally.

"I didn't look but perhaps we had better get back to the hotel before anyone misses us."

"Or my Mother starts to worry, its beginning to get light . . . they will, as you say, start to miss us."

They had driven for about an hour when the truck stopped. "Why did you leave the motorbike?" Sally now asked.

"I thought it might run out of juice," answered Paul.

"Which is what this truck has just done, so let's try the bike?"

They abandoned the truck, removed and righted the bike and Paul kicked it into life.

"If it gives up on us, we'll have to hitch," said Sally as she climbed on the pillion.

And so the tale was told.

"That's it," Paul said, "We've made it." There was a stunned silence, "And we could hear the explosions most of the way home," continued Paul, "even over the noise of the truck's engine. I think, perhaps, there were explosives in those boxes."

"More than likely," said his uncle, "I'll organize reinforcements and you can lead me to this place."

"I haven't had any breakfast," complained Paul.

"Get some now and bring it with you we'll need transport . . ." He rushed out of the office in a determined and purposeful way with Paul meekly following him. "Where did you leave that truck?" he was heard to say.

"Sally pulled up in a lay by, it ran out of fuel, it's quite safe," Paul waved to the others as he departed to find breakfast. "Well, a sort of a lay by," he was saying as he left.

"I wish someone would tell me what's going on," said Annie to Neil as they sat on the beach outside the chalets having seen Sally safely to bed.

Neil looked around, "There is only me," he said, "so will that do?"

Annie sighed, "Don't be so literal, you know what I mean."

"Yes, I do know but as I am addressing a teacher . . ."

"Do get on with it Neil, what's been going on and what are you doing here?"

"To answer the last question first, my only duty here is to escort you safely home."

"You're joking?"

"I'm not joking and I shall take my duties seriously," went on Neil with a smile. "I believe that all this was a misunderstanding. According to Musaba, the inspector you just met, Dr Kimotho was the target and your involvement was exaggerated."

"Don't tell me . . ."

He interrupted the beginnings of an indignant outcry, "I know—you are a teacher on holiday but you see you were involved with Brenda and then Kimani, it may not have been obvious to you but someone put two and two together . . ."

"And made five," said Annie gloomily.

"Sally was unfortunate enough to stumble on the headquarters of a gang that anyone can employ who needs to do a bit of terrorizing, a gang of thugs that Inspector Musaba has been looking for. Once more you have achieved notoriety, you've done it again, unwittingly I know, but that's you. Sally was unlucky, in the dark she's enough like you in size and walk to be mistaken for you."

"Yes, poor Sally, but she is already dismissing the ordeal as trivial." Annie looked at Neil, he seemed upset, "What is it?" she asked.

"She is young and the young take everything in their stride. It might have been worse for you."

"I'm not that old."

"Forgive me, of course you're not. Let's have a swim, I'll get my things."

Sally was much refreshed when she awoke, "What meal is it?" she asked.

"I don't know about you but its supper for me and it's a quiet evening in the hotel, one of those when the guests are told what's on offer. Do you fancy a trip in a dhow, the sea looks calm?"

"What's Neil doing here, is he staying?"

"He's come to escort us home."

"You've got to be joking."

"I'm not and we're meeting him for supper so he can tell you himself. He's got a room in the hotel, the chalets are all booked."

"Have I time for a dip before supper?" Sally now asked, "or is it drinks time?" she looked vaguely about her.

"I'll join you in a dip so let's get going."

"What happened to Paul?" Sally asked Neil when they were sitting and waiting for supper.

Neil told Sally about the gang of thugs. "I don't think there will be any more trouble with those ugly customers with Musaba on their trail. Paul has been united with his family, I think they're all hoping he will get into University over here."

"Are you staying in Kenya?"

"No, I'm escorting you home, I've told your Mother our plans."

"Yes, and what's all this about escorting us and seeing us home, we can look after ourselves," Sally was belligerent.

Neil raised his eyebrows and smiled at this.

"We're going on the train and . . .," Sally continued.

Neil interrupted, "At the moment there are no trains running. We are flying from Mombasa on Friday, that gives you two days to relax after your ordeal. There's been trouble in Nairobi but there's no trouble at the Airport. Your flight is already booked and Dr Kimotho has asked if we will kindly take Brenda back with us. The College is anxious to see her back and term starts next week." Neil spoke calmly, he made it sound so normal and everyday that Sally accepted it cheerfully.

"It'll be nice to see Bob again and we've still time to get a bit of a tan. And Bob can come another time," she leaned over and gave her Mother's arm an affectionate squeeze. "Meanwhile I've got you and we can enjoy it together."

Neil picked up the menu, he leaned back with a sigh, "What are we all having?" he asked. "This one's on me."

It was during this meal that the Manager approached them and asked Annie if she would move into the hotel where it would be easier to guard them. There was an askari on duty in the main block and they couldn't guard all the chalets.

"Then your friend can take over your hut," he explained.

"We've two days left and we don't need guarding," Sally protested, "I wanted a decent tan."

Annie was more accommodating, "It's right on the beach anyway, and if it makes the hotel staff happier I don't see the difference."

"Oh! Ma—I liked that hut," Sally argued.

"You didn't see much of it did you?" she smiled at the Manager, "Yes, we'll move our things."

Sally reluctantly agreed, "We'll be nearer the food supplies—I mean the dining room."

The Manager thanked them and suggested they went on tomorrow's Dhow trip, "No charge for you Madam, it's on the house," he said. Annie thanked him and said she'd love it.

"What about you Neil? Sally will stay on the beach I expect, they'll all watch over her."

"No fear," declared Sally, "I wouldn't miss that."

Neil agreed to go, he managed not to scowl at Sally, instead he smiled at the manager and said what wonderful idea it was.

"Where did those two days go," Sally asked sadly when they were once more at the airport. "I shall come back and bring Bob."

It was on the plane that they heard of the dreadful weather conditions in Britain. It was all very well listening to these weather reports, mentally they were still on warm beaches and the reality when they landed was a decided shock. It was cold and snow was still falling, it was an excellent landing in spite of this and the captain and crew, as the passengers disembarked, were smiling anticipation of some time off. It was obvious that no more planes would take off that day. One did take off, however, a small plane travelling to the Midlands. Annie and Sally managed to get seats on this, they left Neil still pondering on his journey to the West Country where, he assured them, conditions were bound to be better.

At the Midland airport a smallish runway had been cleared.

"But where do we go from here?" asked Sally, she was disappointed because there was no Bob to meet them.

"He didn't know we'd be here, ring him and stop grumbling," said Annie.

Bob had been waiting for a call, he'd hired a heavy vehicle with chains and was shortly with them. The journey was over.

ANNIE'S CASE BOOK

Joy Reid

CHAPTER 1

"**I** DON'T SEE WHY DAN Sleep couldn't make it if you could. He's only in Scotland, you were in Africa!" Maggie complained to Annie.

"You can't be serious," Annie replied, "It was wonderful weather in Kenya, they're snowbound in Scotland."

Maggie had called an emergency staff meeting to discuss whether it would be justifiable to postpone the opening day of the new term in view of the appalling weather conditions which had held up some members of staff. There was also an outbreak of some infection in the town, an infection with 'flu-like' symptoms which was causing some anxiety.

Maggie was still complaining about the absence of some members of staff especially Dan Sleep, the Deputy Head. "I'll never know why he couldn't make it," she went on. "You made it from the airport didn't you?"

"With difficulty—yes, but . . ."

"There you are you see, this will make more work for you."

"Not if we're not here," Annie pointed out soothingly but Maggie was not to be side-tracked. "He said he was stuck in a snowstorm and there were no trains, his middle name is Scott and his namesake Captain Robert walked to the South Pole, so Dan could easily have walked from Scotland. You may not have had to walk Annie, but you came much further than that."

"They were anxious to get rid of us," said Annie reflexively, "this end was the more difficult."

"I don't believe you and I think I shall write a book one day on excuses. To quote Shakespeare and most people don't these days—*often times excusing of a fault doth make the fault the worse by the excuse.*"

"I've certainly heard some good ones in my time," Caroline Boots contributed, "the best ones are usually for not handing in homework."

Everyone present agreed and a lively discussion on excuses was brought to an end by Mrs Gupta, who was also present. "One day given time we should work on it together."

"Yes," said Annie, "time is an excellent excuse."

There were others away not only Dan Sleep. Dawn Johnson-Smith hadn't left Jamaica, Ceinwen Roberts was stuck in Wales, Herr Gebhard said conditions were far worse in Germany where he had spent Christmas with his family.

"Is the weather as bad in Europe?" someone asked and again started off the individual stories and grumbles of all those present. Temporarily the reason for the meeting was forgotten.

"So," said Mrs Gupta, "do we return to school on Monday or do we not?"

"Better put it off for a week, no-one will want to come out in this," said Maggie for it had started to snow again. "We'll put it to the vote."

Most of those present agreed to postpone but Mrs Gupta said, "It is not nice but we are inside and the heating appears to be working, if it were otherwise I, too, would suggest we postponed but we have much to do before Easter and we ought to get on."

Caroline agreed with her, cooking was becoming an important subject and she was longing to start her new programme. Her department was always warm.

But they were outvoted and a postponement was decided on.

"Agreed then, for a week with some objections, Alison—sorry but notices will have to be sent out." Maggie, watching the snow, was beginning to pack up.

"I found an African school for us," Annie wanted everyone's attention but the bitterly cold wind and the snow was of more interest, they were reaching for warm coats and scarves and longing for the time when they reached their own front doors and, hopefully, firesides. No-one showed much interest.

"Another time Annie," said Maggie drawing a woolly hat well over her ears.

"We're still doing Africa aren't we?" asked Annie. "Surely it's just the thing with everyone inside?"

"We'll be needing the hall for indoor games, for breaks and things, we'll get round to it someday, don't worry."

Annie sighed, "All that trouble . . ."

"Trouble!" replied Maggie, "Don't talk to me about trouble, you come back with an enviable tan, from sun, warmth, palm trees, sandy beaches the lot, and talk about trouble! Look at it here, the main road is flooded, rain has turned to snow so it'll freeze over, half the houses in town have leaks or worse and there's this flue-like thing—coughs and colds . . . trouble!" she stumped off.

"She does have a point," said Annie flatly, this was so unlike Maggie. "Nature does seem to be against us at the moment but it won't go on for ever," she finished optimistically.

"I'll close up when you've all gone," Alison said, "I'll get started on those notices. Mind those steps, there's a nasty, icy glass-like patch there."

"Mind the slippery slope," someone repeated in a jocular tone.

Annie turned to see who had spoken, she failed to mind the icy step and fell heavily down the rest of the steps banging her head as she went, she landed with one leg twisted under her and lay motionless.

For a few moments the staff were equally motionless but then someone cried, "An ambulance—call an ambulance quickly!"

"If it can get out or get here," said a pessimistic voice, heard above the general gasps of horror.

Mrs Gupta rushed to Annie, "She will freeze out here," she said, "She must be carried back inside into the warmth."

Mobiles were appearing but it was known to be a blind spot, Alison appeared at the door to discover the reason for the commotion. She rushed back in for the office phone, meanwhile someone had shouted for Maggie who was not yet out of sight. Adrian Lane had also started out but, seeing Maggie turn, now ran back to see if he could be of help. He had been sitting broodily throughout the meeting thinking of indoor games in the football season. An outdoor man, he was also moodily and jealously considering Dan Sleep. How dare he go off skiing and not be able to get back from Scotland; Mrs Hurst was right to be mad about it. Adrian had married recently and they were hopefully looking forward to an addition to the family. Now suddenly Adrian was alive, he was needed, very much so, his training had included first aid and no-one else had much idea of what to do. He was the man of the moment and he blossomed in the role. He could hear snatches of Maggie's phone conversation, she had taken over from Alison. "At the school—urgent—no stone unturned—get here!" as he organized the lifting of Annie.

"Take care of that leg, it's obviously broken and I will carry her," he called out to Alison to make sure that there was somewhere suitable where he could lay his burden.

"She's alive," he reassured Maggie as they carried Annie in. Maggie was still blaming herself; she was full of remorse at having been unkind to Annie, "How could I? What did I say." She was still on the phone—woe betides anyone who made excuses about not being able to send an ambulance or opposing her in any way on the other end of the line.

"We'd better go home," said Mrs Gupta to the still hovering staff, Alison appeared and agreed with this. "I'll let you have news, I promise you." There was a general departure. Maggie having taken over the phone, Alison put the kettle on.

Fortunately the school road had been gritted as had the road to the hospital so it was not long before the ambulance, having picked up Maggie's frantic call, arrived. Anything pertaining to the school was bound to be headline news so they wasted no time.

"The road's in terrible condition—chaos out there," they told the waiting group as they brought in the stretcher. "We'll soon have her in hospital don't you worry," said one of the men. However having checked Annie they accepted cups of hot tea. Adrian was congratulated on his foresight in bringing her inside.

"Never seen anything like it," said one of the men.

"You should see it on North Hill!"

"I told the missus to stay inside, don't want her on the sick list."

"You need to have experience of this sort of thing, now when I was in Norway . . ."

Maggie pointed out that they had to close the school now and that she would accompany them to the hospital.

Tea was finished so Alison, busy as ever, gathered up the cups and told Maggie that she would get hold of Sally. Adrian, unwilling to leave his patient, joined them in the ambulance.

CHAPTER 2

ANNIE COULDN'T HEAR THE SEA or the wind rustling the palm trees and what was that funny smell? Out loud she cried, "Sally, where are you? Oh! Sally, Sally, I've lost Sally."

"No, you haven't," said a familiar voice, "I'm right here."

Annie opened her eyes, tried to move and looked around her at the unfamiliar room. "You're supposed to say *Where am I?*" said Sally.

"Okay, if that's obligatory, where am I?"

"You're in the Herbert Pound Hospital, better know as *Berties* and this is a private room, aren't you lucky?"

"I'm glad you think so," replied Annie with some feeling, "for, whatever happened, it hurts."

"You broke your leg and banged your head, the head has a lot of bandages on it and that thing's the leg." She indicated the raised limb.

"Thanks very much," replied Annie, "And for how long am I going to be stuck in here."

"Until you can walk and possibly until your hair grows back."

"What's wrong with my hair?" asked Annie, horrified.

"I expect they shaved it off, they were more worried about your head. The outside I mean, as far as I can make out, the inside seems to be in working order."

Annie groaned loudly, "My mouth is so dry, any chance of a cuppa?"

"There's some water here, I don't think that can hurt you," Sally reached for the glass.

"You said it was my leg, cups of tea can't hurt legs."

Sally handed her some water. "I'll call the nurse as I was to let them know if you came round. People have been queuing up to see you but its 'no visitors' at the moment." She gave her Mother a quick kiss and departed to break the news of Annie's consciousness.

She returned with a capable-looking nurse. "I'm off to the café, there looks to be a nice looking bar there."

"Its non-alcoholic," the nurse told her in a tone of disapproval.

"I'll bring up a cup of tea then shall I?" Sally tried to sound as if tea was alien to her Mother, and "No G&T then?"

"The trolley will be round soon, it would be easier than carrying it all that way, there are other things on the trolley, newspapers, biscuits, a nice couple run it." said the nurse.

"I've no money," Annie was still bewildered.

"Yes you have, I brought your handbag when I came, there's masses in it," Sally told her. She left to investigate the café.

"Tell me," said Annie to the nurse. "Is Herbert Pound any relation to George?"

"His father I think, they made a lot of money in foundries or something, it wasn't chocolate I know, but they were great philanthropists," the nurse thought for a moment while she checked Annie's leg. "Someone brings books round, if you're interested, there are bound to be some on local history, I'll remind the librarian to call in here. I was there for a time," she added, "at the school I mean."

"Not in my day you weren't," said Annie, thinking she must be nearer my age—well no not quite and certainly not as old as I feel at the moment.

"It was a peculiar place then, had a funny old head, or we thought her old. Not like it is now, it's got quite a different reputation now, I'd send mine there if I had any. I wouldn't do what my parents did—send me to boarding school when they went abroad."

This seemed to be turning into a social occasion with this chatty nurse and not a medical investigation. The nurse continued, "You're a teacher there aren't you?" and without waiting for an answer, "Aren't you the one who found that little boy?"

"Possibly," said Annie, not wanting to start a conversation on her past exploits, "I always thought the Herbert Pound was an old people's home." This ought to get the nurse back on history.

"That was years ago, part of it was a mental home, it's a big modern hospital now, it even has Royal support."

Sally returned, "You still here?" she said brightly.

"I don't have much choice," replied Annie, relieved to see her daughter even if her behaviour under the circumstances seemed somewhat flippant.

"The trolley is just down the corridor, can she have tea?" Sally asked the nurse.

"Don't talk about me as if I wasn't here," complained Annie.

"Yes, fine," said the nurse as she hurried out. "I'll tell the doctor now that I've checked on you. 'Doctor's Rounds' in an hour."

"Why the hurry?" asked Sally.

"To spread the gossip, I expect," answered Annie with a sigh. "I rather think she associated me with past events, I'm tired and I want to be left alone."

"I wanna be alone," breathed Sally in a deep film-star voice (or so she hoped).

"Oh shut up Sally, I don't mean you, but I do not feel like jokes."

"Here's the trolley and another old friend," said Sally as there was a knock on the door. She opened it to the trolley and a kind-looking woman.

"You don't know me," she said, "the names David, I'm Eileen David. You may remember my husband, he's in the police."

Annie acknowledged the connection and friendship, thinking—I've only been in here a day or two at the most and already . . ."—aloud she said, "Sally my daughter will buy me some things. I'm just going to have a rest."

"You do that dear," said Eileen, "I shall be in again. The Bests, Jim and Dot, do this regularly, but I come in now and again to give them a break. They're snowbound today."

"A worthy gesture," said Sally as she busied herself buying all sorts of things from the trolley whether her Mother wanted them or not.

"Also," she told Annie when Eileen and the trolley had departed, "you've got radio which is free, you've a payphone and you have to pay for that fancy television set which swings across. I've already paid something," she added smugly.

"I'd like a bit of a rest now before doctor's rounds, that's bound to be traumatic."

"I'll go now and come back later."

"Is everything all right at home?"

"Oh, yes, absolutely fine, Bob's moved in." With that exit line Sally departed. How very like her to tell me just in that way when I can do nothing about it even if I wanted to; Annie closed her eyes and settled down hopefully to a possible rest.

Next time Sally visited she brought Bob with her.

"Thank you so much Mrs Butcher," he said seriously, "for letting me join Sally at 'The Lilacs', its quieter than the hostel and I'm able to look after her."

Annie didn't tell him that she hadn't had much say in the matter.

"I can't stay; my uncle's here and has something to show me."

"Your uncle?"

"Yes, my uncle's a Consultant Surgeon and it's one of his days here. I'll see if I can find a white coat and then no-one will question my right to be here. I might even find a stethoscope lying around."

"It doesn't say much for security in this place."

"Oh! Its fine," said Bob nonchalantly as he departed whistling cheerfully.

Annie felt it wasn't her worry, her worry was her immovable body, and she turned to Sally.

"How's the weather out there, I can still see snow, how did you get here?"

"The main road is cleared, either that or gritted or something, up here, anyway, so that ambulances can get here. There've been lots of accidents and that private hospital place is closed because of an infection. It's all go out there, lots of people are walking, it's very good for them!"

"I'm sure it is," agreed Annie wishing she was one of them."

"But it's a bit warmer, I believe the thaw might have started."

They were interrupted by the arrival of Dudley.

"How did you find us?" asked Sally. "It's supposed to be *no visitors* yet."

"I can usually find my way about," boasted Dudley, "I said I'd come to service the boilers."

"What boilers?" Annie wanted to know.

"I've no idea but neither had anybody else, so I wandered around until someone told me where to find you. You do look poorly," he said to Annie.

"What! No white coat, no stethoscope," Annie muttered.

Sally was inclined to be indignant, she sniffed loudly, "I haven't had any breakfast yet, I'll go and see what the café has to offer."

Dudley said, "I rang Neil, he managed to get home, it's better down in the west, windy but very little snow. I told him about you so I suppose he'll come soon," he seated himself for a good long chat.

"You didn't have to tell him did you?"

"And if I hadn't told him and he found out some other way—what then? A nice friendship ended."

Annie said gloomily, "Couldn't you have waited until my hair is grown again; Sally says they've shaved it all off, or is she pulling my leg?"

"More than likely, you've enough to worry about I'd have thought without thinking about him. Anyway I can see bits of it poking out from under all those bandages. But if you're worried I'll get Rose to bring you a wig, she'll be coming as soon as she can and when I'm free to look after my beautiful daughter."

"She could always pretend to be domestic staff—the right overall and a mop—possibly."

"Good idea, I'll suggest it," Dudley left.

Am I the only one worried, Annie asked herself, perhaps such trust is justified but if something should happen and the system or lack of it should come under scrutiny? Give the media half a story and . . . hey presto! They'd have a field day. She could imagine the headlines—Students masquerading as doctors, workmen dishing out drugs, porters carrying out operations; even if it wasn't true it made a good story. Annie knew that, having herself being once subjected to it. A simple photograph could be almost anything. She drifted into sleep assuring herself that it was unlikely that anything could go wrong but her dreams included all her friends 'borrowing' an ambulance in order to visit her, and Kevin coming down by way of the roof. If unwanted guests could get into Buckingham Palace and protesters climb over the Houses of Parliament what was to stop a determined visitor from seeing an old friend?

When she awoke she was still thinking of the possibilities and especially of disguise, a clerical collar would surely give right of entry to the wearer, especially if that wearer looked the part. Maggie perhaps in that role or would the idea of the matron (a replacement) be more suitable for Maggie, but Lance—yes certainly Lance as her local Vicar.

These reveries were interrupted by the arrival of the entourage known as 'Doctor's Rounds'. The doctor in charge was unknown to Annie and she was able to relax and enjoy her anonymity. She was just another foolish person who had slipped on the ice. "Progressing satisfactorily, temperature up a bit. Quiet and no visitors." Annie made no comment—she thought that the idea of 'no visitors' a figment of his imagination, perhaps he really thought that his word was law and that hospital rules were religiously kept.

She drifted into sleep again; it seemed to her that she drifted in and out of reality. The next few days were days of comings and goings, she wad dazed and confused, she was determined not to show it but sometimes the pain took over and she relaxed into it. The painkillers and whatever else they were feeding her from a loaded drugs trolley, that seemed to arrive with increasing regularity, were making her feel dopey and unconnected to the outside world.

Sally came and went, trying by her over cheerfulness, to appear unconcerned; this was an extra upset to Annie who recognized her daughter's worry. Dudley was another frequent visitor, he never failed to tell her how ill she looked. One morning he was earlier than usual and she felt bright enough to ask him if he was still maintaining the boilers. He looked around the room as if he suspected if of being 'bugged'.

"Inspector David has been about, he may drop in to see you. Funny business going on, missing drugs and things, they're worried, it may just be the computer system . . ." Annie interrupted, "Ah," she said, "That's how Rose could get in—the computer expert."

Dudley didn't laugh, he looked hard at Annie and with a "See you later," he left.

It wasn't Inspector David who arrived but his wife with the newspaper trolley and gossip.

"How are you dear?" she asked and, without waiting for an answer continued, "It's still me, you see, the Bests find it difficult to get here, though things are better on the roads, a lot have been gritted. Stan, that's my husband, is able to give me a lift as he's working on a bit of trouble up here, there's been some missing equipment and drugs and things, and he thinks it's probably only bad administration or the computer or something. He's bound to come and see you."

Annie thought, 'If they think I'm interested they're making a mistake, the whole system could go haywire for all I care, it's nothing to do with me', she closed her eyes and simply listened. She was roused from this hibernating state when Eileen David continued, "And now," she said, "we hear that this Chief Inspector has arrived. Stan hopes he hasn't been sent to take over his case. I don't think he has, it's not his sort of thing. I shouldn't gossip I know, but there's always gossip in any establishment isn't there? And there's a good deal about this man, I don't expect you met him as he comes from somewhere in the West Country, Bristol or Bath somewhere like that. He had this terrible wife you see, she tried to get into bed with most of his friends, a real nymphomaniac she was. It was, oh, several years ago now, he's a widower, she died of cancer I think. Everybody likes him and hoped he'd have a second chance. Well, what's doing the rounds now is that he's met up with someone, no-one know who she is but he's said to be potty about her and she's playing hard to get or isn't interested or something. The rumour is she lives round here so he may be here to see her and not interfering with Stan. Ears are flapping, tongues are wagging. You can imagine it can't you?"

Annie could, she didn't ask the name of this man, she thought she knew. She asked for a newspaper, making it sound as if she was very bored and tired.

Eileen apologized for gossiping, she changed the subject.

"Your daughter will be coming in to see you I expect, have you only got the one?"

"Only the one daughter, yes, but I have a son, he's stuck in Paris at the moment."

"Paris, now there's somewhere I'd like to visit, perhaps this year, Stan's always promising . . ." she paused but then, seeing Annie determinedly not listening, said, "You don't want to hear me rambling on, I'll see you tomorrow," and departed.

I do hope I wasn't too rude was Annie's guilty thought, was Eileen right and were Neil's affairs a subject for gossip? She was cheered thinking there's one thing about Dudley and his love of mystery, if asked about Neil's *romance* he wouldn't let on. He'd make even more of a mystery with a 'my lips are sealed' attitude.

Should she say anything about it to him or should she rely on him acting in character. She decided on the latter for he would certainly enjoy and make the most of a situation where he saw himself as 'in the know'. She relaxed.

A new doctor arrived with one of the team known as Doctor's Rounds. He was young and breezy and could not have attended the lectures on 'Patient Communication'. He spoke to her as if she wasn't there but when he did address her it was an over-jolly voice, "And how are we today?"

"We're doing very nicely thank you," relied Annie assuming that this was the royal *WE*. She glared at him.

"Eating well are we?"

This fourth-form type really needed taking down a peg or two but Annie refrained, sadly she was in their hands. She glanced at one of the nurses who returned her look and shrugged her shoulders. She replied for Annie saying in a flat voice, "Mrs Butcher finds the menus satisfactory." Annie didn't laugh, she was fairly sure that she would have a visit from this sensible looking woman.

The doctor marked the chart, "Still quiet and no visitors," he said and they moved on.

Doreen Young was more than a sensible woman; she was sensitive, sympathetic and an interested nurse. She came to see Annie that afternoon, she didn't mention any other member of staff—so she's loyal too thought Annie. She had two children at the George Pound School and as well as making sure that Annie was quite comfortable and had all she needed, the progress of these two was also in her mind.

"They speak so highly of you Mrs Butcher and Ian my eldest loves Biology, he would like to do medicine, do you think he has a chance?"

Annie did not feel this was the place for a parent-teacher consultation but two things pleased her, firstly she was not being consulted as a detective and secondly she remembered Ian Young as an enthusiastic pupil who asked endless and sensible questions. So she was able to assure this nurse and Mother, she told her that if Ian continued his progress he would assuredly be able to get into University. *Provided*, she added, that his other subjects were equally satisfactory. Doreen was not, as Annie had feared, an old pupil of hers, the family had moved from Liverpool, Doreen was doing an OU degree and was interested in administration.

"I'm on duty now so I must go but I'll come in later before I go and see if you want anything."

Sally arrived at this moment, she was delighted to see her Mother looking so much brighter.

"Who was that?" she asked.

"A good nurse, a parent and, I hope, a friend."

"So, if you're okay d'you mind if I get a swift snack in the caff? I told Bob I'd meet him there, is there anything you fancy?"

"I'm well looked after thank you, there'll be another trolley, possible food, along soon."

Sally opened the door, she said, "Oh! Hi!" to the man hesitatingly standing there, she turned back to Annie, "It's Inspector David, shall I let him in?"

"Of course," replied Annie.

Inspector David had easily found Annie's room, there was Dudley to show him the way as well as his wife. He was very sympathetic, he read her notes and commented on her case, "You're healing nicely," he told her.

"Thank you" said Annie with a laugh, "Perhaps you're in the wrong profession."

He was puzzled by this and seeing her more cheerful looks told her of improving weather conditions, a thaw was forecast.

"Things will soon get back to normal," he said. "Already the roads are clearer and people are getting about." Annie indicated a chair and he sat down. "I hope my wife didn't tire you," he continued, "She does like a bit of a chat you see, it gets a bit lonely now that the children have left—well they're no longer children—and you know how it is."

"It's called *empty nest syndrome*," Annie told him.

"Really! I'll tell her, she'll like that. This job is giving her a bit of a break. The Bests don't like driving in this weather and I come up fairly regularly, I can give her a lift. I'm looking into some suspected thefts here—lots of stuff missing," he paused. "If you do happen to hear anything . . .?" He got up and walked up and down.

"Perhaps I'd be better in a general ward," Annie suggested.

They were interrupted by the arrival of the lunch trolley, earlier she'd marked a menu and was now surprised to find that she was quite hungry and looking forward to this meal. Inspector David left her to it.

She was settling to a rest when Dudley reappeared. "Do you work here permanently now Dudley?" she asked him.

"There's always things to be done in a place like this, I'm keeping a look out for Inspector David, he's been to see you hasn't he, what do you think?"

"I hope all these people here don't think I'm a detective Dudley. I'm a teacher as you well know. I'm not interested, not a bit, in the troubles here. It's their lookout and I'm not a bit surprised. How this place survives at all is what surprises me."

"So you do know something?" Dudley was all ears. Annie gave him no encouragement.

"It's my rest time," she told him and resolutely closed her eyes.

Sally came as he left.

"For anyone not allowed visitors I'm not doing too badly," Annie said to her.

CHAPTER 3

ANNIE WAS DELIGHTED TO WELCOME Maggie, it was a bright cheerful morning, there was still snow to be seen but it had a gleam to it not a grey slushy look.

The visitors ban had been lifted. A senior doctor had looked in to her room where Sally and Dudley were drinking coffee and a porter was sitting on her bed.

"Not much sense in saying *No Visitors*," he commented, "If it's allowed you'll probably have fewer." The porter had sprung to his feet not sure whether to salute or not.

"Sod's Law," agreed Dudley, "I'm off anyway," he retreated in what Annie thought was a cowardly manner. Sally stood her ground muttering about 'Mother'. The doctor advanced into the room leaving enough space for the porter to slip away, he hoped unnoticed.

"So you're Mrs Butcher," said the doctor.

"I'm afraid so," said Annie.

"I knew Bernard and I think I met you at his funeral."

He looked familiar thought Annie, so she smiled.

"Alright, visitors again," and "I'll see you later." He departed with a satisfied *I've found you* look.

Sally said, "Coffee I think," and also left.

Maggie arrived soon after this.

"That was quick," Annie exclaimed, "They've only just lifted the visiting ban."

"Sally said it didn't make any difference," Maggie replied. "She said there was no trouble getting in, everyone did it and you were in a private room anyway so it didn't matter."

"I thought it was *No Visitors* for my health not for everybody else's convenience," Annie protested. "And I'd rather be in a bigger ward, there's more going on!"

"I expect one of the reasons was so that you could be available to your clients, you're rather well known you know."

"Maggie, how could you, you know I have no clients, I'm a teacher," once more Annie protested.

Maggie laughed, "I can always get a rise out of you that way. So—how are you? I came to ask that and to bring cards and flowers though I see you have plenty."

Annie had hardly noticed them, there were always flowers and cards in hospitals, now a feeling of guilt came over her, they were for her and people had gone to all that trouble. "When Sally gets back I'll get her to write some 'thank you' notes, it will give her something to do in the café."

"Does it still hurt?" asked Maggie.

"Yes, and I'm told I may always have a limp."

"It'll make you more interesting, all sorts of stories will circulate, they'll ask 'What was the old Butcher doing to achieve a limp', and you could carry different sticks from all over the world," Maggie expanded on her theme.

"Forget it, talk sense. How are things in the outside world?" Annie enquired to bring Maggie back to earth.

"We're opening on Monday if, by the outside world, you mean the George Pound. The thaw has started and the roads are mostly clear. I suppose floods will be the next thing. Most of the staff are back. Dan Sleep and Dawn have made it and Helen will be here soon I believe. You'll know that but I'm sure Joel has been trying to be with you. Have you heard from him?"

"Only through Sally. They've got a flight at last, there was trouble on a runway in Paris."

"We shall miss you," Maggie meant it.

"A good topic of conversation," Annie told her cheerfully.

As Maggie was leaving she remembered that Lance had asked her to see if their friend Clare Hanwell had visited Annie.

"I don't think so," said Annie, "Is she likely to have done so?"

"Well it would be easy for her, she IS the Matron, a modern Matron."

"The Matron!" Annie exclaimed, "Are you sure?"

"Of course I'm sure, newly appointed but, yes, she's here. You may remember her—very musical lady is Clare. She used to help Lance organize concerts or lectures for young people. Lance speaks very highly of her. I think she's a bit of an archaeologist as well—she's very talented. She's been working for the county I think but was very much hoping to get this appointment. Well—she's got it."

"Yes, I remember vaguely, she was at one of your parties, most interesting, she'd been in India hadn't she? I'll look forward to a visit."

"I'm surprised she hasn't been yet."

"There's been some sort of trouble," said Annie reluctantly.

"Trouble, what sort of trouble, that's what hospitals are for—trouble."

"This is missing stuff, equipment, drugs and things; Inspector David is here."

Maggie shook her head knowingly but she said nothing as she gave her friend a parting wave.

The porter appeared to be an old friend by the time he managed to find Annie on her own. He had not only pushed her around on her arrival but managed to slip in with any other trolleys. Annie began to feel she knew him, he was another white coat always very fresh and clean. Maybe he helped in the laundry too. He was always smiling and cheerful but apart from knowing that his name was Luke and was Nigerian, she knew little about him.

"Now," he said, "I hear you help people."

Annie was about to deny this but she was curious.

"Not when I have a broken leg and am lying in bed in hospital."

"But you are able to give advice?"

"But surely there are proper authorities to give advice?" she answered.

"Yes, oh! yes, but I am an illegal immigrant," he told her, "and everyone says you help them all the time."

She was disbelieving.

"Me?" she enquired, "Are you sure?"

"They say that you even rescue them from the sea when they try to come into this country that way."

"They are pulling your leg."

Luke looked at his leg obviously puzzled!

"It's only a saying," Annie explained while thinking—this is an impossible conversation and situation, is this what is meant by my interviewing my clients. She thought for a while before asking, "How did you get here?"

"I always walk, even in the snow."

"I meant . . ."

"You mean how did I get the job at the hospital? Oh that was easy, I answered an advertisement, I have lots of papers with stamps on, they are short of strong young men," he answered proudly.

"How did you leave Nigeria?"

"I caught a plane," he explained as if to the simple minded.

"If you caught a plane you came in legally."

"Oh!" he said disappointedly, "Can I not be an illegal immigrant?"

Annie tried to explain the difference as far as she was able. "You came here as a visitor and stayed?" she questioned.

"I have a cousin in Birmingham. He said to give his name, he has been here many years, he told me how to get the papers with lots of stamps on them, he said that over here that was all they wanted. Then I get this job, I like it here and then I meet this girl from my country. I want to stay; we shall marry and have babies."

"I'll give it some thought," Annie promised. Why Oh why can't I just say I can't do anything Annie asked herself. What I will do is to mention it to Inspector David next time he comes and then forget about it. It's just not my business.

Inspector David agreed with her, he was not sympathetic towards the young man.

"If he paid his fare then he is not poverty stricken, I'm not sure I believe all the tales of danger and torture in their own countries. However if he has a good job here with equally good references and if he has relatives here willing to vouch for him, I don't think there'll be any problem. I'll enquire anyway just to stop you worrying when your worry is about getting better and getting out of here."

Annie laughed and thanked him, she enquired into the hospital troubles only to be told that so far he had made no progress.

"Did I hear you wanted to be in a general ward?" he asked, "because if so you could keep your ears open—gossip—you know and things." He finished on an enquiring note.

"Why not," replied Annie thinking that the move might be interesting but not necessarily good for her health. Perhaps that hadn't occurred to Inspector David.

"A nice wash dear?" was one thing Annie dreaded, she had been worried at first that the nurses might be old pupils and however pleased she might be to find that her biology lessons had not be wasted, she feared that 'washing the old Butcher' might be worth a few giggles. But two of the nurses she now know as Hazel and Nicky were helpful, gentle and called her Mrs Butcher. They treated her with kindness and respect which she appreciated.

Hazel said, "Have you met the new Matron?" when they had started on their task and being careful not to hurt her. Annie replied that so far she hadn't had that pleasure. To say she'd met her socially didn't seem necessary.

"She's a bit of an old cow," said Nicky as she washed an arm.

"Really, in what way?" asked Annie, half concentrating on her wash and only half listening.

"She stopped Janet Lucas taking some Ibuprofen for a headache."

"She did take six or seven lots," Hazel added. Janet does overdo it a bit."

"Well why not? There's plenty, she didn't know how long the headache would last did she? Hanwell didn't need to make such a fuss."

"But there's always something wrong with Janet, she does seem to need an awful lot of vitamins and did she really need something for malaria?" Hazel was doubtful.

"Which is Janet," Annie enquired now very much awake.

"You may not have seen her, she's on a geriatric ward in the other block," Nicky told her.

"We do need things," Hazel explained and the dispensary isn't much help either.

"What sort of things?" Annie tried not to appear too interested.

"Janet took that di . . ." Nicky began.

"Shush," Hazel protested and added for Annie's benefit, "the girls do need things—you know—its obvious isn't it?"

Annie began to think that Clare Hanwell might be justified in tightening up on dispensing.

"Does it strike you as being a trifle dishonest?" she tried not to sound accusing, just interested.

"No," said Nicky, "they owe it to us, nurses survive on a pittance, everyone has perks, and it's well known."

"Not a pittance surely? I thought . . ."

Hazel interrupted, "We can manage but if it's possible to get a bit more who can blame us."

"And Harry will always take any extra, he paid for drinks for a month when Janet got hold of . . ." Nicky was again interrupted by Hazel, "Someone forgot to lock the drugs cupboard I think. Dr Stevens hushed it up, the doctors can get anything they don't have to sign for it."

"This Harry sounds a bit mean, where do you meet him?" Annie asked casually, she gave a small cry of pain to take the girls' minds off the fact that they were gossiping too much.

"Oh! He's always at The George, it's a good pub, and a lot of us go there."

"Does Harry work here?" Annie wanted to know.

122

"No, but he comes and goes like—well sort of but not while that snooping Dudley is about, he and Harry don't get on."

"Oh! sorry Mrs Butcher, did we hurt you? I think he fancies Janet."

"Who? Dudley?" Annie was disbelieving.

"No, Harry," Nicky sniggered, "certainly not Dudley."

Annie was relieved, she couldn't see Dudley in the role. She reassured them on the cry and said the pain had gone.

The wash was over and the nurses with a cheerful 'see you later' left Annie with her thoughts.

She felt depressed. Of course Inspector David had to hear this but she felt that this new Matron had the drugs affair under control. The last thing Annie wanted was to get these girls into trouble but then the thought came to her. Perhaps it was done on purpose, perhaps it was their way of letting the authorities know that things were not right in the drugs department. Perhaps even now they were discussing among themselves and asking if she had taken the bait? They might even dislike this Harry or have got it in for Janet. The situation was full of possibilities, one thing was sure—it was Inspector David's 'case' and he must tactfully deal with it.

She fell asleep.

It was teatime when Bert appeared. He was in working clothes and carrying his tool kit. He dumped this down saying, "I don't let it out of my sight, expensive these days tools are and you never know . . ."

"Do you work here Bert?" Annie asked him.

"I've kept the place going," Bert answered proudly, "and now, with the thaw, there'll be burst pipes, drains blocked, you name it, it'll happen, there's so much to do, Kevin's been helping me and that friend of yours, Dud Russell, he's here too." Bert sat down.

"Do you think all is well at 'The Lilacs'?" Annie asked him.

"Don't worry, Dud'll tell me if I'm needed. You're not to worry, just get better again, everyone misses you—there's Kevin now?" he paused on a questioning note.

"Oh! Please tell him to come, he knows about hospitals, we can compare notes."

"Kevin 'ud enjoy that and Alf too, would you see Alf?"

"Of course."

"Only that policeman friend of yours . . ."

"You mean Inspector David?" Annie interrupted.

"No, the other one, the one with the posh name and he . . ."

"Annie interrupted again, "It's not particularly posh, if you're interested in the origin of names, it's probably originally French," Annie thought she sounded very schoolmistressy so to lighten her outburst she added, "Your name may mean that an ancestor played the harp."

"Harper," Bert roared with laughter at the thought, "I'll tell Kevin, we could take it up."

Annie laughed too, thinking how cheerful Bert was these days and how much fitter. She brought him down with a bump, "How's your sister-in-law these days—Kevin's Aunt Ag?"

Gloom settled on Bert again but it didn't last long.

"As I was saying—that friend of yours brought us some money to smarten Alf up a bit. He said we were entitled to compensation for Kevin's being beaten up that time but Kevin thought that was unlikely and he really wanted Alf to visit you when the weather was better."

"Interesting," put in Annie.

"So we went to the charity shops and you should see the things we got, Alf don't know 'isself, we got him a suit and new trousers for Kevin and snazzy pyjamas for them both?"

"Pyjamas?" questioned Annie, surely this was a very liberal interpretation of Neil's ideas and probable generosity.

"Well, you never know," said Bert, "It is a hospital and Kevin was in one up there some time, long enough to wear them out.

"Did you say Kevin is coming to see me?" she now asked.

"Yes," Bert looked about him in a sheepish sort of way, "he's got something to bring you."

"I shall look forward to it," she told him. Do I mean the visit or the mysterious 'something' she asked herself.

The Matron Clare Hanwell came in as Bert was leaving.

"Plumbing problems in here?" she asked.

"Bert was just reporting on my own home," Annie explained, she felt guilty but saw no reason why she should.

"So all's well," Bert said to Annie giving her a conspiratorial wink as he went.

Annie remembered Clare Hanwell who was very upright and dignified; Annie knew little about her other than that fact that she was a friend of Lance and Maggie. They had talked about India where she had been Matron of a hospital in Delhi. Annie was pleased to see her again, they spoke of their mutual friends—the Hursts—after Clare had reassured Annie as to her continuing to make good progress. Then she said, "This is a very special request and you may well refuse. We have a case, a woman who definitely needs a room of her own. We're so busy, we have nothing available . . . I wouldn't ask only Inspector David said that he was sure you wouldn't mind—in fact that you had even mentioned . . ."

"Yes," said Annie, "I did say that I should be quite happy in a small ward if that was possible, I believe he said he was investigating some missing equipment."

Annie told herself that nothing, but nothing, was going to get her involved. I'm here with a broken leg and a massive headache and in **no way** . . .

Clare Hanwell interrupted her thoughts, "Of course we have everything under control but we did think we ought to inform the police and Inspector David is so discreet. We are all very careful, of course, but we are willing to have someone about, we don't want to be accused of secrecy."

Did she really think everything was under control, thought Annie, she let it pass. She had already indicated her willingness to move. In spite of her determination, she suddenly had one of her 'prickly feelings'. Why was Clare so anxious for this move?

Clare went on, "We should not, I know, bend our rules in this way because of a noisy, demanding and I must admit philanthropic husband—well yes—he has given much to the hospital, that Chemotherapy Unit for instance. I shouldn't let personal feelings come into administration but he can also be a nuisance in a public ward. It just happens that Mrs Morris was discharged this morning so there is a bed in 'Kenilworth' Ward. If we could move you then Mrs Harbottle . . ." she paused.

They were interrupted by a knock on the door and Nurse Young, looking angry and frustrated, half entered the room, she was pushed aside by a large, aggressive red-faced man.

"Yes, this will do," he growled belligerently, this woman's only got a broken leg as far as I can see, when can you move her?"

"Matron, I'm so sorry," pleaded Nurse Young. "Mr Harbottle . . ."

Matron stood her ground, "It's only if 'this woman' agrees," she said firmly. Mr Harbottle retreated before her, Annie was glad to see. Nurse Young gave Annie a look of despair and departed after them. Annie almost laughed only laughing hurt.

Matron returned, "Mrs Butcher, what can I say—if you've changed your mind?"

"Oh! No, I shan't change my mind," Annie said and to herself, 'I'm in this whether I like it or not.'

"Nurse Young sent her apologies, she's very upset," said Clare, she was hovering, "I'm not allowing myself to be bullied but you can see for yourself what he would be like on a general ward and we're still not sure what's wrong with his wife."

"Sally, my daughter won't like it, and neither will Maggie, but we'll give it a go." **GO** was the operative word, thought Annie, just go and let me rest a bit, for before long everyone would be at her, Dud and Rose as well as Maggie and Sally, all saying 'Why did you let them?' And she couldn't say 'why?' it was just that something—perhaps Dudley would understand?

She was moved into Kenilworth Ward that evening.

CHAPTER 4

ANNIE SLEPT BADLY. THE MOVE was just before supper and caused some agitation among the inmates of the ward, questions poured over her and she tried to give answers to 'why did they move you', 'didn't you like where you were', unhappily she said she was better but fully aware that she felt a good deal worse. Fortunately supper put an end to the questions; discussion of the food then took over, it being of greater importance. As each bed had a television a popular soap absorbed everyone's attention when supper had been removed.

Annie feigned sleep but her pain had increased. She wanted to ask for stronger painkillers but did not wish to draw attention to herself, during the night she regretted her stupidity.

Next morning Sally arrived in an indignant mood, she drew the curtains around Annie's bed which made little difference to the loudness of her voice.

"Of course I'm mad, why ever did you let them? I barged into your old room and there was only a ghastly woman in your bed."

"In what way ghastly?" asked Annie intrigued.

"Terrified I thought, what has she got to be frightened of here—I ask you?"

"Do lower your voice," Annie implored, this is a ward where everyone can hear." Annie was almost whispering, she didn't want to stir things up again, she was supposed to be—well what, incognito? In any case she didn't want general attention again. She tried to explain in a low voice that Inspector David was hoping for some help.

"Ma, you're impossible, quite impossible, I thought I heard you say you wouldn't get involved and I won't be the only one whose mad, everyone will be and that Neil, who arrived and is staying with Dud and Rose, he'll be furious."

Annie's mind was elsewhere.

"Do you think you could accidentally barge into my old room a few more times? The husband was a horrid man, I'm sure he has something to hide. You could keep forgetting that I'd been moved, did that woman look ill or only frightened?"

"What should he be hiding and why is she in there anyway?"

"That's what I was hoping you'd find out."

"He's probably got a bit on the side back home."

"More than likely, especially as one of the nurses doesn't think there's anything wrong with her."

"She's probably in for tests, I'll ask Bob."

Bob was intrigued and a bit mystified. "Can I be in on this?" he asked.

"On what?" Annie enquired, "There isn't a '*this*' yet," she added after a pause.

"She isn't involved," Sally told Bob with a sigh, "she just can't keep her nose out of things."

Annie was indignant, "I'm just sorry for anyone who has to live with a pig like that."

"She doesn't have to, Ma, this is a free country with people to help, she can walk out."

"Okay," said Annie, "I'm only suggesting you keep ears to the ground and eyes open. Of course Bob could pop in now and again in his white coat."

"Don't worry, we'll watch out and we might hear things in the café—coming Bob?"

"Is it always open, you seem to keep it going?"

"Oh" Yes, and it's a hotbed of gossip," Sally triumphantly left the ward followed by Bob."

A doctor appeared, he seemed to be in a hurry, "Has anyone seen Mr . . .?" he stopped short at the sight of Annie and asked angrily, "Who gave permission to move you?" It was against my explicit instructions, what was Matron thinking of . . .." Still in a hurry he rushed out still muttering, Annie caught words as he went down the passage, words such as "Wait until I," and "Harbottle you," and "What tests."

So someone else doesn't like that man thought Annie as she watched his retreating back and collision with Eileen David and her trolley.

"What's the matter with him?" asked Eileen. "What's he on about, seems in a bit of a hurry. Someone dying in here?" she laughed at her own joke. No-one else did.

Annie said as Eileen approached her, "It's my move that annoyed him, but your husband wanted me here. Where is he by the way?"

"He's got a bit of a cold, he drove me here so he's not too bad but he didn't want to spread it, especially not here." She pushed the trolley round the ward, chatting and selling. One patient, Pam Addison, was expecting to go home and was waiting, hopefully, for the time when her husband could get his car out, she was complaining bitterly about the weather.

All conversation stopped when Luke, the porter, arrived bursting with news and excitement.

"I went to your old room," he told Annie but addressing the whole ward, There was a nasty, very nasty man in there, he called me a f---ing black bastard and said I shouldn't be here. But there he is wrong," he was jubilant, "I can be here, my papers have come, she did it for me they told me she would, she is wonderful," he waved his papers, pointing to Annie.

Annie tried to protest, she tried to point out that it was impossible for her to have done anything in the time. It was no use, he continued to tell everyone how marvellous she was. Annie gave up and added her congratulations to the general applause, for Luke was a popular man, and they joined in his happiness.

"I shall get qualified," he told them, "and become a nurse like on the telly."

He met a friend at the door of the ward, they could still hear his voice and his praise of the wonderful Mrs Butcher. This friend now came in, it was Kevin. "He says you got him a work permit, he'd been waiting and waiting but one word to you . . ." He was smiling as he came up to Annie.

"Nothing I say makes any difference," said Annie. She now noticed that Kevin was carrying a large and heavy suitcase.

"Are you staying long, Kevin?" she asked him, a long weekend perhaps?"

Kevin was now used to her style of humour and merely grinned. "Dad said you'd like to see me, made a joke about playing the harp. You always manage to cheer Dad up. He didn't tell me they'd moved you, there's not much room in here is there?"

"There's plenty of room for a bed, a cupboard and a chair, what had you in mind?"

Kevin indicated the battered looking suitcase. "Alf went shopping, Dad took him because he wanted to buy you a book, something nice to read as you were a brainy lady, he kept turning over all the books and in the end they found this old case and loaded it up for him. He only had to pay for the one, they're rather more than he bargained for." He indicated the battered suitcase.

Annie was amused as she visualized the scene.

"I didn't know they'd moved you," he repeated. He sat in a dejected way looking down at his feet and clasping his hands.

"What is it?" Annie asked, she knew her Kevin. Recognized by everyone else, though not by her, as her sidekick. Not by her, as she steadfastly denied her involvement as an investigator.

"There was a funny woman in there," he replied.

"How 'funny'? What did she look like?"

"Well," he looked up, "not like you Miss." Annie laughed.

"Was there a man there?"

"Yes, he was just coming out, he told me to get lost."

"Ah-h-h." Annie was momentarily lost in thought, "and the 'funny', you haven't said, how funny?" Sally had said the woman looked frightened. Now if only Kevin would define funny she might be able to form a picture, she felt he ought to be able to come up with a description with some meaning. She waited while Kevin pondered.

"She looked very unhappy, she didn't look pleased to see me, she'd been crying I think, she didn't like the man, there was an atmosphere—it was horrid. "Should I go back?" he asked, "when the man isn't there?"

Annie wondered if there was a white coat big enough to fit him, she swallowed the suggestion that he should look for one.

"Why not," she said, "Let's give it some thought."

"Kevin brightened considerably, he felt that they were again in it together and that he was part of the team.

"But now," said Annie, "we must consider what to do with all these books, it looks heavy, you don't want to take it back again and I shall enjoy looking through them when I'm back in my old room. There must be somewhere where you could store them—just temporarily."

"Isn't that woman staying long then," Kevin asked.

"She's just in for tests, or so I heard. Could you come back later Kevin, at a time when everyone is watching a favourite soap?" Annie didn't think anyone was listening, they all had visitors but you never knew. "You could then tell me what you've done with the books," she added.

"I'll find someone who knows."

"Isn't there a general office, an administration centre, a place where you could ask?"

"I haven't seen one, it's the weather, people are ill or stuck somewhere, they're very short staffed and the Matron is new, no-one seems to know anything and she doesn't seem to know anything either—or so Dad says," he finished lamely.

"Who's running the place, or don't you know?"

"Dudley—I think."

"Dudley?" Annie couldn't believe her ears. "Dudley?" she repeated, "surely not, or are you joking?"

Kevin laughed but didn't reply.

"I'll tell Dudley to come," he said as he left the Ward, now I'll see if I can find some storage space."

It was quite late when Dudley came, he, too, disapproved of Annie's move.

"Inspector David had no business to suggest this," he grumbled, "he asked me to keep an eye on things—I ask you—what can you do in bed with a broken leg?"

"I can listen, it was Matron, too, who agreed with the idea, she wanted a single room for the wife of a benefactor."

"I've heard all about it, it's very fishy."

"If you use that word I am immediately on the alert," said Annie brightly.

"Bert and I have got ourselves a little office, there's a man called Dennis who's been here ages, he uses it too as do the ambulance men, they use it for tea and coffee making, we're very cozy there."

"Does Matron know?" Annie was amused.

"She hasn't discovered us yet but she hasn't much idea of who is who and who should be where. Berts a useful bloke, he can always say he's looking at the plumbing. This Dennis does all sorts of outside jobs, he's been helping us look for some sort of storage. We've got your books safe in our office."

"Thank you very much," Annie said trying to sound grateful.

"This Dennis," continued Dudley, "is also a useful kind of bloke. He says the oldest part of the building which isn't new, is due for demolition. He says it used to be a loony bin."

Annie, disapproving, said, "An old people's home surely, that's what I'd always heard."

"That's not what Dennis says, he says there are lots of bricked up and sealed up places, he tells some hair-raising tales, he says you wouldn't believe some of those walls . . ."

Annie interrupted, "No, I probably shouldn't believe it, do you?"

"Oh well," Dudley agreed, "but it livens up coffee time. Tomorrow we're going to explore properly, Kevin thinks it'll be good fun."

"I'll be interested to hear what you find in these buildings, keep in mind our real investigation."

"We'll do it thoroughly, I promise you," he could see she was tired and after pointing it out to the Ward Sister he said 'Goodnight' and left.

Annie was tired and asked for some more painkillers, she felt too tired to sleep but did eventually fall into a restless half-sleep and half dream-world. During the night someone brought her a pleasantly warm bundle—ummm—a hot water bottle of sorts. This must be some new sort of treatment—cuddly toys, stroking animals, excellent idea, it was working. It comforted her and she slept peacefully at last.

She awoke to the sound of a crying baby, it was far away—no—it was very near, it came from her own warm bundle.

I thought, she observed to herself, I am in here for a broken leg! Anyway this appears to be of Asian origin and . . ."

Someone was standing over her, it was Nurse Young staring at her in horror. She took the baby from Annie who repeated aloud her own observations. Nurse Young didn't laugh.

"And I was off duty, you must have heard something . . .?" she was almost accusing.

Annie became aware now of the general unrest about her, agitation and hassle, she could feel the disquiet. Matron was among the throng that now gathered about Annie's bed and other occupants of the ward were protesting that they had heard nothing until the child cried.

Matron addressed them all, "Someone, in the night, swapped all the babies around, we have them in the nursery in order to give the Mothers a rest, they were all in the wrong cribs, all the Mothers are in tears. There was only one missing, this is it." She finished triumphantly.

Nurse Young, still holding the baby, rushed back to the Maternity Ward.

CHAPTER 5

DUDLEY, BERT, KEVIN AND DENNIS had chosen the wrong morning for their search, after a brief consultation they decided that baby swapping had nothing to do with them and they would be better out of everyone's way. They set out to the different part of the building that Dennis had described and where he assured them many distressing scenes had taken place. He enlarged on this until Dudley, concentrating on his own detective role, told him to 'shut up'. Dennis did, probably because he had run out of suitable horrifying words. He bore Dudley no ill will but went on to describe the use of various disused parts of the building. It was a dark and gloomy building of a rusty looking red brick, crumbling now and ripe for demolition. It was deserted and looked as if it had been so for some time. They walked round it and told each other of the possible plans for this extension to the hospital.

Kevin wandered someway from the others and his sudden shout drew their attention. "Look!" he shouted, "Look here." They joined him, all staring at very recent tyre marks. "It was snowing the night before last, these are fresh!" The others agreed and Dudley knelt down wishing he had a magnifying glass. He had no need of one, even

Holmes himself could see that, these marks were very obviously fresh. They looked at each other as Dudley rose from his knees, brushing off the snow.

Dennis looked extremely puzzled. "A fairly heavy vehicle, how did it get here?" he looked all round and started to follow the tracks.

"Where was it going?" asked Bert.

"Why was it here?" put in Kevin.

They followed the tracks which led to a fence put up between the old and the new. It had been broken down and now a rough, temporary structure had been erected where the permanent fence had once stood.

"Don't go too near," waned Dudley, "there will be footprints and the police may want to see them."

They returned to the old building.

"There may have been footprints here too," pointed out Bert, "but we've stomped all over them."

They were wondering what to do next when Kevin again shouted, "Look, look here!" and the others joined him by some steps which led down to a large door. Kevin had descended the few steps and was gazing at the lock.

"It's newly oiled," he told them, "but we haven't the key, it looks as if it would be an old heavy one."

They looked at each other, they decided to return to their 'office' and Bert volunteered to hunt for the key. In 'their room' Dudley put the kettle on while Bert went on his errand.

Dennis and Dudley drank their tea in silence. Kevin, not interested in tea, decided to go and tell Annie of their doings, he felt she shouldn't be kept out of things.

"We've been exploring," he said to her, "in the old buildings . . ." He told her just what they had found.

Annie said, "I think you'll find that your door wasn't opened last night unless of course they had a duplicate. I heard that Matron collected up all the keys in her drive to stop this disappearance of drugs and equipment. She locked them up in her office and probably has that particular key on her. Find your father, he'll think of a way of getting at them. Once he sees them, a big old newly oiled one should stand out.

Kevin found Bert outside Matron's office, he too had discovered where the key was to be found. But where was Matron?

"I can't find her," he grumbled.

"She's in the Maternity Ward smoothing the Mothers, I just saw her," said Kevin. "I suppose it isn't really funny," he added, "but there was such a commotion in there but luckily no press." He then went off to the coffee shop to get himself a drink, here he found Sally and Bob. Sally appeared to be running the place.

"No-one was here," she explained, "I got the key from Matron who has started a security drive. She told me to get on with it, everybody seemed to be in a panic, and we're keeping well out of it."

"It seems to be all babies and keys," said Bob. "I'm not sure what's going on."

Kevin said, "We, Dad, Dudley and me, are looking for a key too. Its one to a curious outbuilding, it's being used for something and there was a lorry there last night, I'm confused as well!"

"Did you see Mum?" asked Sally.

"Yes, I did see her and I think, by the way, she was muttering about a diversion, that she had a theory, she was deep in thought when I left her."

The woman who usually ran the café now arrived apologizing for being late, Sally handed over the key and with Bob and Kevin left for what she called 'The Action'.

'The Action' was taking place in Matron's office. Her thoughts and concern were mainly for the babies and anxious mothers. Who could be responsible for such a trick, surely not a joke, if so what a peculiar sense of humour. However no actual harm seemed to have been done. Now she was faced with another problem. She faced it with a 'don't-bother-me-now' attitude. But Bert the plumber was not to be put off and was trying to tell her a story of a locked door in some outlandish place and the absolute necessity of finding a particular key to fit it.

"Why?" she was asking him as Sally, Bob and Kevin joined them, "why do you need to get into this peculiar place just at this moment?"

Dudley now joined them, he had come to discover the reason for the delay, he backed up Bert and told her, "We have to get in there and I think you should come, Inspector David would have wished it." He wanted to make it clear that he was deputizing for the police.

Sally added, "Mum thinks there may be a connection between the two events." She wasn't at all sure if this was true but it startled the others and helped the Matron in her decision. She found some possible keys but it was Kevin who, as they all peered at them, was the first to pick out the big old-fashioned and recently oiled key. "This is it," he cried out positively, as Annie had told him what to look for.

Dudley slipped away, he felt he must find Dennis to lead the way and tell stories of past horrors. He found Dennis who had been joined by Luke in their 'hideout'. Luke was enjoying a quiet coffee but had no intention of missing any excitement so he, too, was part of a now largish group.

Kevin, who still had the key, led the way followed closely by Dennis who was being encouraged by Dudley to tell some of his more lurid tales.

"Where are we going?" asked Matron. "Where on earth are we?"

"It's the old building Ma'am," Dennis told her, "the old Loony Bin."

"How dare you use such a term," objected matron. "I don't believe a word of . . .," she looked up at the old decaying building, " . . .it's dreadful," she finished.

Kevin still had the key and it was he who descended the steps and fitted it into the lock. It turned easily, the door was no problem for the hinges had also been oiled and it opened inwards without even a creak. His cries of surprise brought the Matron to the fore of the group (or was she pushed?). Dudley had been showing her the tyre marks.

The door led into a large dark room. "I need a torch or something," Kevin turned, "We need light, has anyone got a torch?" he asked unhopefully of the others who had started to join him, there appeared to be a large number of boxes in this semi-cellar. No-one had a torch.

"Let me go in," said Dennis, "there may be something they've fixed up."

"Who are *they*?" asked Sally of no-one in particular as Dennis pushed past Kevin and found some contraption for light fixed up, no doubt to help whoever had dumped the boxes.

They all went in and walked round what appeared to be a large room, thick walled and with no light save that of Dennis' find. There were boxes of all shapes, sizes and descriptions mostly marked 'Medical Supplies' in large lettering.

No-one spoke and even Dennis was silent, stopped in mid-sentence with talk of dungeons, as he recognized the gravity of the situation.

Matron was aghast at the sight, she gasped out, "What the—who—who—if—why?" in short terrified words. No-one answered her.

After a while speech came back to them. Matron turned on Dennis, "So what is all this?" she enquired accusingly.

Sally answered for him, "You're the boss," she said cheekily, "you tell us."

Matron was not pleased but to say she hadn't been there long enough to realize the extent of the buildings only sounded like lame excuses so, although she glared at everyone, she was silent as she examined the various boxes and packages. It was obviously meant for the hospital and it was very much in the wrong place, such as a derelict building due for demolition. She was the only one there who had seen the new plans, she felt she should have known where the new buildings were to be situated.

Dudley said in a matter-of-fact voice, "This is what Inspector David is looking for, I'd better let him know even if he isn't well."

He went outside to be sure of a good signal. Inspector David, coughing and sneezing, thought that it would be unwise to come, "Stay there," he said, "I'll get onto headquarters. Don't worry, I can deal with it." He wasn't interested in baby swapping and he told Dudley that he thought there was no connection.

Dudley returned to find everyone trying to guess the contents of this 'haul' which they were all busily examining. He told them of Inspector David's comments.

"I don't agree about the connection," protested Sally. "If Mum thinks there is one there probably is, it could be a diversion." Both Dudley and Kevin agreed with her, they trusted Annie's theories.

Dudley and Dennis agreed to watch over their discoveries, taking alternate shifts. "In case one of us freezes to death," explained Dennis with relish. The others returned to the main building to await developments.

The excitements of the day had left Annie very tired and irritable, lunch had been a hurried affair and there had been no after lunch nap, everyone had been gossiping, nurses had been coming and going to tell their part in the drama or merely to tell of various theories and speculations. Dudley and Kevin came (separately) to tell of the thrills in the cellars and to ask if she really suspected a tie-up between the two events. Such different events but yes, possibly one to distract from the greater crime.

"Of course," said Annie, "You'll see."

Matron did not come, Sally explained that she was too busy 'marshalling her troops'.

Sally, too, told of the discoveries in the disused and derelict building, she and Bob had had a good look at the packages. Dudley, she told Annie, had sent for Rose to sort out the Hospital computer system, she thought some of the equipment had never reached the main building, other packages had possibly been added to the growing accumulation.

"And last night was the night for its removal," suggested Annie, "and what has she done with Victoria Grace?"

"She's been fussed over in the nursery," Sally laughed, "but she was asleep as I came by.

"There's a police woman looking into the baby case," Sally went on, "she says she knows you, I can't remember her name but she was very shocked when she asked after you and heard that you were in here as a patient. She'll undoubtedly be coming to see you, so far she's been busy taking notes from anybody who'll collaborate with her, or who likes the sound of their own voice," Sally finished cynically.

Later that evening Annie was not surprised after Sally's news to see her old friend Sergeant Tracy Williams.

"I was on leave up here," Tracy told her, "visiting some old friends and this awful weather prevented my getting back. Mother says it's worse there." Annie remembered that Tracy lived with her mother.

"Then Inspector David, he's got a filthy cold, heard I was here," Tracy went on, "he's got permission for me to stay here for a bit and look into this silly baby business, baby stealing he called it, only there hasn't been any stealing, could be a practical joke, only it isn't funny. I've been working on real baby smuggling—now that really isn't funny, I've been out to Romania. I think I've been forgiven, do you remember?"

Annie did and asked after possible promotion. "It's on the cards," Tracy told her, "and I shan't false step again." She laughed, "Inspector Williams, can you imagine it?"

Annie congratulated her and told her friend that she deserved it, she did think so but wished she'd go away.

"Oh, and do you remember that other Inspector or was he a Chief Inspector? I hear he's about too but he's more interested in all these stolen goods."

"I think I know who you mean," replied Annie cautiously.

Tracy said, "There can't be any connection can there? I've talked to so many people, they all think the baby thing is an inside job, funny in a not funny way but everyone was somewhere else. Have you any idea who can have done it?"

"Oh yes," replied Annie.

At that moment a nurse came round with tablets and to see that the ward settled down for the night. She came over to Annie, doled out her medicine and made sure she was comfortable.

Tracy was contrite, "Here's me rambling on, you must want to rest, you don't look yourself at all." She pressed Annie's hand and made for the door, she paused and returned. "You said you did know who did it?" she asked.

"Oh! Yes, Mrs Harbottle of course, and don't ask, TELL her she did it and ask her why?"

Annie closed her eyes in a dismissive way.

CHAPTER 6

TRACY WAS AT A LOSS, completely empty of ideas, the only one being that she had no idea what to do. If it had been anyone else but Annie Butcher she'd have laughed it off, but everyone had complete faith in Annie. Tracy decided to find someone to advise her but when she joined the obviously involved group around Matron's office she found that the subject under somewhat heated discussion was the amazing discovery of all the missing equipment. They were totally wrapped up in the affair of this unsolvable mystery.

Dennis had disappeared before someone started to throw the blame onto his shoulders. His suggestion of blowing the whole place up had not been well received.

Tracy knew that this was not the moment to return to the baby problem and that her news would fall on deaf ears.

Dudley meanwhile had rung Rose and insisted that her knowledge of computers was essential and that she was to get a taxi and come as soon as possible. She was there now, she had gently pushed aside the young man sitting in front of the computer, he had been engrossed in the instruction book and appeared to be terrified of the screen as well as the various knobs, keys and attachments. He gave way thankfully to Rose and went to find his coat with hope of a quick getaway.

Rose was getting on with the job of finding out, if possible, when the delivery or different deliveries had taken place, who had authorized it, if anyone, who had received it, if at all, and why, oh why had it ended up in a disused cellar. If it had been brought there and dumped then by whom and by whose authority.

Nobody knew anything, the Matron least of all. Tracey was glad to see a familiar face of a man standing quietly a little way from the assembled company. Surely, she thought, this was the Inspector she had known when she worked up here, the one whose case it was involving smuggling of illegal immigrants and the murder of a small boy (see "*Annie Butcher's Jigsaw*"), she couldn't remember his name, La something, ah, that was it, LaCoste.

She approached him now, "Do you remember me Sir, Sergeant Williams?"

"Of course I remember you Sergeant, it's nice to see you again, is everything all right with you?" he spoke kindly.

"Oh, Sir, tell me what to do," she told her tale, he was not dismissive, he listened and was interested.

"Mrs Butcher was so sure, she said not to ask her but to challenge her with it—the 'we-know-you-did-it' approach."

"Oh! Did she indeed?"

"What do you think, Sir? What shall I do?"

"Nothing tonight Sergeant, its late and night-time routine is in operation. I'll have a word with Mrs Butcher myself and we'll think about this Mrs Harbottle in the morning." He had no idea about the identity of Mrs Harbottle.

Tracy was content with this, the burden was lifted from her shoulders and when he suggested a coffee, if the café was still open, she was more than content, it certainly wasn't the time to discuss it with Matron.

Neil had brought Rose in, he had answered the phone when Dudley rang, (he was staying with them) and offered to drive Rose in and not to wait for a taxi. He had been listening to all the hospital troubles when he saw Sergeant Williams approach him, he had been watching Rose, he approved of her quiet serenity when she was on the job, no-one was deflecting her from her task and even Matron was relaxing a little.

After listening to Tracy he beckoned to Sally who with Bob was also admiring Rose at work. "Is the café open do you know?" he asked her.

"I don't expect so," replied Sally, "but I'll reclaim the key and open up, we could do with something, couldn't we Bob?" She turned to Bob who thankfully left the others and said, "Yes please," with a grin. Having found the key the four of them set off for the café. Tracy was disappointed to find that it was not a tête-á-tête, especially when she heard Neil address Sally by her Christian name. Bob was feeling that he had missed out somewhere so he detached Tracy from the other two and insisted on hearing her story and exactly what Annie had said.

Neil saw his opportunity, lagged a little behind the others and asked, "How is she?"

"Not well, one of the doctors, Dr Khumar, is very worried about her, I try to keep her reasonably cheerful but I was furious when they moved her."

"Moved her, why?"

"I think it was Inspector David's idea, hoping she might hear things, he's on the case of missing stuff, too many drugs disappearing as well as all those other goods. She's in a general ward, Mrs Harbottle is in her old room."

"Ah! Mrs Harbottle again."

"Can you do anything?" Sally pleaded, "She doesn't need to hear things, she needs to get well."

"I agree and I'll see what I can do."

Sally thanked him and indicating Sergeant Williams who, with Bob, was some way ahead of them said, "She fancies you, you know."

"I'm not on the market as you well know."

"I wasn't sure but I don't blame you. She'd love to see you I know, but not tonight."

"Sergeant Williams told me that the ward had settled down for the night and I have no wish to disturb her," Neil paused, "Tomorrow then?" No name was actually mentioned but they each knew who they were talking about.

"Tomorrow will be fine I'm sure," Sally reassured him, "I'll get in early and make her presentable."

"She'll always be presentable, as you call it, to me, you know that."

Sally smiled up at him, "but I have to warn her, we don't want her temperature to go up and she'll want to look her best, I know that when she said I wasn't to let you near her she really meant . . ."

He interrupted, "But surely if . . .," he was distressed.

"Don't worry Neil, she's only worried about what she looks like, isn't that a good sign. Some of her head bandages have been removed now, I told her they'd shaved off all her hair so she was a bit worried, but it wasn't true, I was only trying to make her lie still and let it grow again."

"I never knew that lying still was necessary for hair growth."

"Well, you know what I mean."

Neil smiled, "I think I do," he answered her.

They arrived at the café, there were several people including two nurses peering in and looking hopeful so Sally was greeted them with enthusiasm. She opened up confidently and started up tea and coffee machines as well as dealing with the bacon rolls.

Neil wondered what her role was at the hospital, "Just a volunteer, that's all," she told him cheerfully. He was reluctant to leave the subject of their previous conversation but as they had now joined the others he managed to continue in a less personal way.

"You mentioned a Dr Khumar," he said to Sally, "Is he any good?"

Bob interrupted, "Very good, I should say, I like him a lot, he's very conscientious. Trained at Barts I believe, but he does have this belief that everyone's against him which they're not. I think he's wrapped up in his work and his patients and anything outside that passes him by. Present goings on are only causing him confusion. He doesn't realize it's only temporary."

Sally said, "It isn't only the weather although Dr Khumar hates that, I think this place was always a bit of a nightmare. The new modern Matron has no idea what she's taken on, it's a bit like the George Pound School before Mrs Hurst, Maggie, arrived, I'm sure you heard about . . . well this place must have been the same. One thing I do know about Dr Khumar, he was dead set against moving Mum as was Dr Brierly—but now—perhaps," she looked at Neil who got the message, she added, "You know what they say about a drop of rain falling on a stone?"

"Yes," he replied, "It can take hundreds of years, I am not prepared to wait that long." Sally laughed. The others, having no idea what they were talking about, took the conversation back to the weather, finished coffee and bacon rolls, and waited for Sally to shoo everyone out and lock up again.

When they got back to Matron's office it was to find that Rose and Dudley had gone. Rose thought that she was on the way to interesting discoveries; she would come again in the morning. "Don't anyone touch it, she had said as she closed down the computer. "I'll put a guard on it," said Matron. Although Rose was worried and didn't trust anyone nothing would keep her from Victoria Grace's feeding and bath-time, she left messages for the others as she and Dudley left.

Tracy thought it a good time to tell Matron of Annie's suspicions of Mrs Harbottle. Matron looked doubtful, after some thought she said, "We can but ask, alright, I'll come with you, but not tonight, we'll go in the morning."

Tracy had difficulty next morning starting her motorbike so that she arrived late at the hospital, she went straight to Matron's office. Here she found not only Matron but also two doctors, Dr Brierly and Dr Khumar, as well as Superintendent LaCoste. Earlier Neil had sought out the two doctors, he had been at his most austere and relentless in advising the immediate removal of Mrs Butcher to a private room.

"I couldn't agree with you more," Dr Brierly said, "Dr Khumar and I were very much against this move to a general ward. Mrs Butcher is not doing as well as we should like, she is often feverish in spite of antibiotics and other drugs, I'm not a bit happy about her and am glad to have your support, Dr Khumar feels the same."

Matron was on the defensive as Tracy arrived. It wasn't my idea," she was protesting. "Inspector David wanted her where she would hear things, she has done, of course, but she is not in here to do work the police should be doing, its not surprising that her temperature is fluctuating," she paused for Tracy was trying to get her word in.

"As I was saying," continued Matron emphatically, "Not only did I have Inspector David on my back but that horrible Mr Harbottle insisting that he and his wife were privileged persons having given so much to the hospital."

Rose heard this, "Oh! Have they," she exclaimed. "We'll see about that, exactly WHAT have they given, and if so where is it?" She was indignant, why should anybody, however generous, have precedence over her friend Annie. The computer would reveal all, she couldn't wait to get to the truth.

Tracy's mission was to see Mrs Harbottle, Matron had promised to go with her.

"Mrs Butcher was so sure about the baby business, sure it was Mrs H." She was determined.

Matron spoke to a passing nurse, "Do you know if Mrs Harbottle has had breakfast?" she asked.

"No Matron, I looked in on her but she was asleep, I decided not to disturb her."

Matron turned to Tracy, "I feel sure you're capable of dealing with this yourself, you don't need me," she said firmly, "no bullying mind."

"I'll come with you," said Sally, "To see fair play. I know the way. I was off to the café but Bob's not back yet.

"Good," said Matron, "Now we can sort out the business of where to put your Mother."

Sally and Tracy left, Sally leading the way to Annie's old room. She knocked, there was no reply so they both went in, Sally went over to the bed, "Time she was up anyway," she said to Tracy, "I don't believe there's anything wrong with her."

She bent over the bed, Tracy joined her and gently pushed Mrs Harbottle onto her back. "I believe she's dead," Tracy said in a hollow voice. She felt for a pulse, "Feel!" she said to Sally.

Sally felt, "There isn't one," she acknowledged. "I believe you're right."

Tracy was an experienced police officer but even she was shocked and uncertain what to do.

"May I point out," Sally told her, "that we're in a hospital. We'll leave it to the experts. Not only that but the place is full of police, so let us rejoin the nerve centre of this pile and relate our news."

"I am the police," said Tracy as she led the way.

Their news stunned the occupants of Matron's office. Dr Khumar, the youngest there, went first and fast, the others were not far behind. Neil stopped the general exodus. "Stay here," he said as he followed Dr Brierly, he blocked the doorway, "the fewer the better for the first investigation and diagnosis." The others waited in heavy silence, looking at each other.

"I know what I'm going to do," said Sally, "and that's opening up the café. Come on Bob."

"I think I shall resign," said Matron.

"You've only just come," Sally protested, "It wouldn't be appropriate."

"I'm a modern Matron," said Clare, "If I want to resign I shall do so."

"Okay," said Sally, "Coffee anyone? Come on."

CHAPTER 7

"I CAN'T SIT HERE DRINKING coffee," Tracy complained to Sally. "As I pointed out earlier I AM in the police force."

"Then undoubtedly you'll be called back on the case especially as you found the body," Sally retorted. "So go if you feel you should but as for me, I'm keeping well out of it. I shall go and tell Mum soon if she hasn't already heard, she probably expected it anyway. I'll take her some coffee as the drinks trolley people seem to have deserted and Mrs David has probably caught the Inspector's cold." She heard a group of nurses already discussing the news and sat at their table as Tracy departed.

"Who is she?" one of them asked, "Seems odd dying like that."

"This is a hospital," Sally said. "Surely people die sometimes?"

"Not here they don't, its discouraged," said another with a humourless laugh. "The policy is to send them somewhere else if they look like packing up on us." She sniffed loudly.

"Sister Watkins said there was nothing wrong with her," a dark girl looked puzzled.

"This'll be a shock to the new Matron, it looks bad," said the original speaker.

"And she moved that nice woman out to put this one in."

"Just as well perhaps," put in Sally, "And I'm going to take that nice woman a cup of coffee, please mind things. I won't be long."

Matron had given up her idea of calling a meeting of the staff to tell them of an unexpected death. Rumours had already spread with surprising speed and the meeting was unnecessary, perhaps not so surprising as Dudley had disappeared on a mysterious errand. Rose was already engrossed on the computer.

Tracy hovered, uncertain what to do, when Dr Brierly came into the office, he was in a very sober mood and he shut the door quietly. "I am very sorry to have to tell you, Matron, but there is no doubt, Mrs Harbottle has been smothered. We shall have to wait for the post-mortem of course but the Superintendent agrees with me," he paused, "this looks like murder."

"Before I do anything else," promised Matron to anyone who was listening, "I'm going to find somewhere for poor Annie Butcher, it would be the last straw if . . . "

Dudley entering the room overhead this and interrupted cheerfully, "No problem now is there? She can have her old room back."

Matron gave him one of her most withering looks as she left the room but she made no comment.

"You can't be serious," protested Rose turning from her work on the computer.

"Well," Dudley responded, "they'll soon move the body and all they have to do is to clean it up a bit."

Rose's look was almost as blighting as that of the Matron but Dudley was not one whit put out, "I don't see why not," he muttered, shrugging his shoulders and smiling at Dr Brierly who was standing quietly in the background.

"Aren't you a Special?" asked Dr Brierly, "because if so I think the Superintendent would be glad to see you, he has other things to do and would like to set the wheels going."

Thus dismissed Dudley went willingly to be welcomed by Neil. "This is not my case as you well know, Dudley," he said. "Stay here while I find someone else until Inspector David comes. His cold must be better by now, there are plenty of his people about, I'm going back to make sure Annie isn't forgotten."

"Nice room this," said Dudley. "You go and get things moving. A dead body's nothing to me."

Clare, returning to the office and speaking more to herself than to anyone present, said, "Perhaps I shall stay after all, its possibly what a modern Matron has to put up with, it certainly isn't dull. Why shouldn't an odd job man be running the hospital and the daughter of a patient the café? Stolen goods hidden in a falling-down outbuilding and now a murder—it's all vital and lifeblood to a modern Matron. And now," she continued, "its nothing to have an Italian woman shrieking in the corridor."

"Oh!" said Dr Brierly, "is that what the noise is? How long has she been here?"

"The ambulance men just wheeled her in and left her."

"Where are they?"

"I've no idea."

Neil now joined this indecisive group around Matron. Tracy was there, worried about sitting in the café when she felt she ought to be somewhere else.

"I'm glad you're here," Neil said to her, "for Inspector David says you are to take over the enquiry into this woman's death. He will be coming as soon as he can find someone to keep an eye on his wife, she isn't well having caught his cold. He won't be long and has already been on to your division to ask to borrow you for a time." He indicated his mobile.

Tracy blossomed, she was happy again.

"The Inspector says that providence sent you," he told her, "so over to you."

Tracy departed, quite ready to take over until the Inspector arrived.

Dudley now reappeared determined not to be 'bossed about' by Tracy who he knew from an earlier time when she had worked in the area. "Who's making all that noise?" he asked.

"An Italian woman who arrived unexpectedly," Matron explained. "The ambulance men have abandoned her so we've no idea what's wrong with her."

"Oh! I know where they are," Dudley reassured her.

"Good," smiled Matron, "but first of all we're going to move Mrs Butcher into that pleasant little store room I've found. As there don't appear to be any stores we might just as well make use of it. Then we'll put that noise into Kenilworth Ward and the doctors can look at her."

She turned cheerfully to Dr Brierly, "I know," she continued, "that the present occupants of the ward won't like it but I can't help that. We've no other vacancies except one bed in Maternity but I'm not putting her in there!"

"Dudley bent over Rose, "Stores?" he asked. "Any news?"

"When I get a bit of peace round here," replied Rose, "I might be able to tell you."

"But now," said Matron firmly and addressing Dudley, "can you find me a porter and we'll move Mrs Butcher, a nurse too, if you can see one."

Dudley looked down the corridor and saw Luke leaning on the wall, he didn't appear to be doing any portering so he gave him a low whistle, Luke joined him, the shrill racket of the protesting Italian woman could be heard echoing around the corridors.

"She has some good swear words," Luke explained. "I was listening."

"But surely they're in Italian."

"Not all of them, some of them very good, strong, meaty words."

"No time now to listen, we're going to move Mrs Butcher into a small room near Matron and then put that female into Kenilworth, you should hear some more meaningful words from the other occupants of the ward, they won't like it one bit."

"So when do we move the wise and wonderful woman?" Luke asked. "I am ready."

The 'wise and wonderful woman' hadn't slept well, she seemed, even to herself, to be slipping backwards down a slippery slope. She heard someone say, "It's snowing again", which made things worse. She wanted to be well, to be home, (and where was home). Home had a garden and she wanted to be in it with the sun shining; instead of which the pain enveloped her, her head ached, everything was miles away or muzzy. To add to her discomfort a new disruptive noise infiltrated her brain just as she was sliding into an uneasy dose. Italian words broke in on her and she was with Bernard again, on a holiday first in Rome and then in Pompeii where she worried and worried about the damage tourists were making in the ruins. The language broke in on her semi-dreams, she was asking Bernard where the person making the racket came from. "What part of Italy?" she asked. "That's not Italian at all," Bernard was saying, "She's play acting, pretending, amateur dramatics, what play is it? It's funny, funny and fishy." His voice faded away and the 'fishy' sounded more like Dudley.

Annie became aware that there were people around her and she awoke.

The activity around Annie had started in Matron's office, the comings and goings had some purpose. Rose, however, was not on the move, she stuck to her post with a grim determination to get to the truth of why the missing paraphernalia should be housed in unused crumbling back premises, as well as where missing drugs had gone? Or why had they gone? Or . . . there were many possibilities.

Dr Brierly left briefly to make sure that the loudly complaining patient wasn't about to have a baby which appeared to be one of her laments, other insisted ailments being a broken ankle and appendicitis. "She isn't even pregnant," he said when he returned, "I've instructed Sister Watkins to give her a sedative, perhaps that will quieten her for a time, there's no broken ankle and no symptoms of appendicitis. Now . . . Mrs Butcher?"

"So you've fixed that Hullaballoo, permanently I hope," said Dudley cheerfully. He and Luke were at the door impatiently waiting for the 'moving of Annie' party. Sally, who had closed the café, joined them.

From some dark part of the hospital Kevin appeared carrying a very large bunch of flowers beautifully wrapped. Matron looked suspiciously into the darkened passages beyond him; there were other parts of the hospital where she felt she had still not ventured. Kevin knew he should be in school and had a slightly guilty look but he told himself that no-one here knew that and he could always play the part of plumber's mate. He was able to convince himself that, with more snow falling, nothing much would be happening at school, added to this his father's talk of 'goings on' further convinced him that this is where he should be. He'd wished he'd brought something for Mrs Butcher as he'd heard she wasn't too well so he'd been down to the 'hide-out' to consult Dennis. There he found his father and the two ambulance men as well as Dennis, tea was brewing.

"No problem," said Dennis. "Wait here." He returned shortly carrying a very fine bouquet.

"There you are," he said triumphantly.

"But—but—they must cost . . . where did you get them. I'm afraid I—I?"

"Always plenty of flowers about," explained Dennis. "Patients don't always want them, give them to the nurses, nobody knows whose is whose anyway. Did you want any chocolates?"

Kevin was momentarily speechless, Dennis took a fine piece of wrapping paper from his overall pocket, "Waste paper basket," he assured Kevin as he arranged it tastefully around the flowers.

The procession was just starting out as Kevin approached the office, Dudley saw the flowers.

"There are enough of them going on the rescue party, let's wait in the room Matron has fixed up," he said to Kevin and turning to his wife added, "Come on Rose, leave that and join the welcoming party."

"Eureka!" exclaimed Rose.

"What do you mean?"

"I think," suggested Kevin, "that she's found something."

"I think at last I've got it—Eureka—eureka!" Rose was jubilant. All the same she agreed to join the welcoming party. "Pity we haven't got a banner," she said.

Afterwards Annie always asserted that her recovery started when she opened her eyes and saw her extra large pupil and self appointed 'side-kick' with an apprehensive face half hidden in flowers. Could he be going to a funeral? The thought that it could be hers aroused her and started her mental progress to recovery.

She had been in pain and full of her own woes when the rescue party had arrived. The changeover was soon made and the still protesting Senora Massarotti wheeled into Kenilworth Ward. Annie allowed herself to be manoeuvred and moved into her new quarters.

Matron said, "You'll be nearer to me, that ward is too far away—an advantage if the senora starts up again."

Annie had no idea what she was talking about, someone was holding her hand in a comforting way, Sally was there and above her she could hear Luke still singing her praises. It was then she saw Kevin.

"Kevin," she said, "tell them he did it." For some reason her brain was suddenly clear.

"He?" queried Kevin, at a loss.

"The husband of course, Mr Harbottle, he murdered his wife."

CHAPTER 8

"**B**ETTER GIVE THIS WARD A name," said Clare as she prepared to make this pleasant little room a home from home, she was bringing in the tea things.

"May I suggest *Lilac Ward*," Annie agreed, "that's the name of my bungalow, I'd feel at home then."

"Good idea, I expect Dudley will fix something up. It's quieter in here than in my office," she indicated the tea-making equipment. "Also we must see that you have all the other things—phone, radio and of course the telly so that we can watch all those hospital soaps—then all our own excitements will seem quite ordinary."

Someone had put Kevin's flowers in a vase but he was still standing just inside the door.

"Lovely Kevin, thank you, but shouldn't you be in school?"

"Mr Lane said not to bother, he said he thought I'd be doing more good here. Then I could help me Dad and I could take news of you back to him, then he'd spread it in school."

Annie thought kindly of Adrian Lane, she'd heard how good he'd been when she had had her accident, however, this . . .?

Kevin continued, "He's been very good to Alf too, brings him things and sits with him, he's nearly always there when Dad and I get in so's he can hear all the news from here. I don't think he's much in school either, says it's a free-for-all, nobody knows who will get there, and it's confusing he says." It sounds it, thought Annie.

"Is Mrs Hurst there, or is she ill?" Annie was concerned. She hadn't heard from Maggie. These tales didn't sound like Maggie.

"I'll find out," replied Kevin. Sally came in and as he left he added, "I'll tell the Inspector."

"Poor Adrian," said Annie, "I don't think he likes indoor games. I'd like to see him; can you get a message to him? I should have asked Kevin."

"What are you talking about?" asked Sally. "Your mind is wandering. I'll get you some tea." She saw that the tea things were on hand. "Oh! How thoughtful, you can rest now and I'll keep the world at bay."

This proved to be an impossible task, Matron had moved herself in declaring that it was 'quieter in here'. Nurses and Doctors naturally visited but Sally did tell Inspector David to 'come back later'.

The Inspector was somewhat put out by this although he agreed to it. He felt a little triumphant although he had no intention of crowing over Annie. She couldn't always be right, of course, but her theory that Mr Harbottle had killed his wife was obviously wrong. He had a cast-iron alibi. This alibi was a most respected man living in the Cotswolds and he and his wife had no hesitation at all in stating that Mr H had been staying with them. This is what he wanted to tell Mrs Butcher but, 'yes', he would call back later. Maybe her mind had been wandering or Kevin had got it wrong. No matter, he was full of confidence.

"They're guarding you well," said the nurse Annie knew as Hazel when the two nurses, the other one being Nicky, came in for the daily wash. They had been very subdued for the last day or so but now they obviously (to Annie) had something to say other than the comments on her progress.

"Even Dr Khumar, who is generally so pessimistic, and Matron are talking about a Zimmer frame."

The very idea horrified Annie but she knew it was a beginning and she agreed that she was on the mend at last while she waited for them to unburden themselves in their own time.

"We were all interviewed," Nicky said.

"Good, what did you tell him?" Annie enquired.

"It was HER."

"Right, what did you tell her?"

"Nothing, we don't know anything," said Hazel.

"Its surprising," Annie suggested kindly, "what we know when we think we don't."

"And Janet kept a low profile," Nicky added.

Hazel took a deep breath, "Would you see Janet, she doesn't want to push in and she thinks Matron's got an eye on her?"

"Couldn't she come in with the next meal? Surely one of you could organize that?"

'What is this?' thought Annie, 'I'm not a prisoner, I'm a patient. Also I'm a teacher and I'm agreeing to something odd from a teacher's point of view.' But was it odd? She had yet to find out.

"And come back later yourselves," said Annie firmly, "I want a bit of a chat."

"We will," said Nicky.

Sally arrived at the same time as Annie's lunch. "I came to tell you that the thaw really has set it, did you know your Neil has gone?"

"Yes, he said a brief goodbye, he had to go back to his own patch but he'll manage a weekend soon."

"Good, I'm only here briefly, Bob's with his uncle now, then we're going to see what's happening at Uni." She noticed the nurse still standing there holding a tray. "Better have your lunch," she winked at the nurse, "You've got her going at last—see she eats up. See you . . ." she left to join Bob.

"Are you Janet Lucas?" asked Annie, the nurse nodded. "You wanted to see me," Annie continued, "Can you stay a while?"

"I heard you did so much to help people, everyone knows about you, even one of the porters can't stop talking about how wonderful you are."

'Here we go again,' thought Annie. Aloud she said, "People exaggerate, I'm a teacher, I teach at the George Pound. Were you one of my students?"

"No, but that big Kevin's one of yours isn't he? He said to come to you, wouldn't do any harm he said as you were so discreet and you'd know what to do. I dunno—I—" she burst into tears.

Annie pushed her tray aside, "Please don't," she said soothingly, "someone is bound to think I am being cruel to you or, worse still, Matron might come in."

Janet dried her tears, she was almost smiling and already calmed by Annie's manner and attention.

"It started with Harry, he was always at the pub where some of us go on an evening off. It's a quiet place and we can have coffee if we don't want to drink. I thought I liked him, he was very attentive, he was a bit old but my Grandma used to say 'better an old man's darling than a young man's slave'."

"That's a bit old-fashioned, in those days a girl's only career was marriage. So you liked this Harry?" she asked.

"He was always bringing presents and buying drinks, it was later he asked us to bring him things, the more expensive drugs if we could get them."

Annie remembered that Hazel and Nicky had spoken unflatteringly of Harry. They said he'd buy anything they could get hold of. Didn't they speak of malaria tablets? Maybe he was thinking of hiding away in a South American jungle? So was Janet trading with Harry? It looked like it. And what else was involved?

"I think I'm pregnant," sighed Janet.

We're getting there thought Annie. "Then you're in the right place if you want to get rid of it."

"My Mother will kill me," Janet was starting to sniff again.

"I doubt it, Mothers come round in the end, maybe even offer to help," Annie paused, "maybe she was reared by your grandmother's principles," she added.

"He was absolutely horrid," Janet continued after a minute considering Annie's remarks. "He said it was my fault and that if I was capable of getting hold of all the stuff he wanted then I was capable of looking after myself. He hit me and said he'd tell everyone, he'd expose me—I hate him now, how could I have been so stupid?"

"Matron will have to be told, you know, she certainly won't kill you although she may question your choice of mate. I'm sure she'll help."

"The girls know and they've told Sister Young."

"And the result?" Annie questioned knowing that Sister Young would be a sympathetic listener.

"They all say the same but he made me. He said I'd end up in prison."

"I doubt it, I think you weren't the only one helping yourself, security was very much at fault."

"Its better just talking to you but I know I did wrong." Janet thought for a while, "I think I should tell you that it's possible Mrs Russell, the new computer technician, has found out something. I heard her say something to Dudley, do you know Dudley—they may be related? Anyway she was saying about Harry and he was replying that he'd met a Harry in the pub and he wouldn't trust him further than he'd throw him—fishy he called him."

She paused for breath.

Fishy? Though Annie, that's Dudley. I'll have a word there. What am I thinking of. I keep telling myself not to get mixed up in anything. She groaned at her own weakness.

"Are you alright?" asked Janet, "I didn't mean to tire you."

"I'm fine," replied Annie. "I'm just thinking, I always groan when I think."

"You're thinking that I only came to you because it was being found out anyway and I wanted . . ."

"The idea never entered my head," Annie interrupted. "You're not still with him and you're not taking the stuff now, this all happened some time ago didn't it?"

"I never liked doing it, yes I stopped ages ago, well—not ages—but sometime, that's another reason he was so angry, he'd booked in at a hotel because I said I wanted to see him. He thought it was to bring him another load when I wanted to tell him my news. I tell you, he was furious, called me every name under the sun." Janet's tears were very near again.

Annie asked, "When was this hotel booking and would they remember?" *Am I possibly on to something,* she wasn't sure but listened carefully for the reply.

"It was only a few days ago, I remember exactly because it was the night that poor woman was murdered, it let me out of the questioning because I wasn't there you see."

Annie's only thought was 'what a good alibi' but why should Janet need one? Annie hadn't touched her lunch.

"I'll fetch you another one," said Janet.

"Don't bother," said Annie, "I'm not hungry." There was a knock on the door; Janet opened it to Inspector David.

The Inspector was far less confident when he now managed to see Annie. Interviews around the hospital had proved to be inconclusive and unconvincing; he felt that there were too many people involved. On conferring with Sergeant Williams he found that she had come to the same conclusion. Nobody seemed to know anything, to have seen anything, or heard anything. Or was it that if they had they had no intention of talking about it.

"Perhaps we could get them for non-cooperation with the police," she had suggested unhopefully.

"Not a very bright idea, a lot of good that would do." The Inspector was dismissive.

Tracy was about to say that it had been meant as a joke but she realized that he was not in a joking mood. "Shall I have a word with Mrs Butcher?" she suggested instead.

This thought had crossed his mind but no way was he going to admit it. "I've searched other leads," he told her, but to himself he said, "I wish I knew what they were."

But here he was at last, Annie gave him a welcoming smile which immediately dissolved his reluctance to discuss his difficulties with her. Here was a friend, a friend whose brain he respected, whose quiet confidence he admired and of whose integrity he had no doubt. She was someone who understood people, he had no secrets from her.

He had begun to suspect that the superintendent's relations with her might be a little more than a casual friendship but who could blame LaCoste if it were true. He kept to a formal approach and said, "we don't seem to be getting anywhere with this murder, your idea that it was the husband was quite out for he has a cast iron alibi."

If Annie thought he sounded a little smug she didn't say so, she knew she wasn't always right. "A cast-iron alibi?" she asked. "That's suspicious in itself, would you know where you were two weeks ago on a Thursday night, but tell me about it, often talking to someone else brings unexpected light."

"He was staying with a friend in the Cotswolds, he said he was taking advantage of his wife's stay in hospital. Knowing that she was being well looked after gave him the opportunity to visit old friends who would vouch for him. The police up there were very co-operative, they said he was still there but I believe he has returned now to see to the funeral arrangements. They've released the body now. By 'they' I mean the big county hospital, 'they', too have been most co-operative, all tests and the post-mortem were done there, they've better facilities, of course. Sergeant Williams and I were left with all this interviewing business, it's been very trying and doesn't seem to have got us anywhere," he finished with a sigh.

"So I heard," said Annie.

"What have you heard?" he asked brightening up.

"Surprisingly, as I am now in a secluded corner near to the Matron, quite a lot. Do you remember (see '*Annie Butcher's Jigsaw*') when we last worked together we called it a jigsaw and then suddenly all the pieces fitted together. I think the same will happen here."

"Perhaps," he said.

What am I saying thought Annie, I'm talking as if I am Miss Marple or Sherlock himself—I'm a teacher. Nevertheless she continued, "What I think now is that you have an obvious suspect with a so-called cast iron alibi. His victim, I also heard for nurses talk, is covered in bruises; for a start get him on that. If he's that sort maybe he's been cruel to the RSPCA cat and the RSPCA will back you."

"There's been no mention of a cat," protested the Inspector, to himself he considered that to upset her theories was one thing, to replace it with another was far more difficult. Where to start, and she could be right! A different aspect worried him, he put it to her.

"Even if it had been possible for him to get here from the Cotswolds, the weather being as it is, or was—it's thawing now—the idea of his getting in here is ludicrous, the security . . ."

"Is very lax as you well know, a white coat, possibly a stethoscope and away you go."

Inspector David was shocked but had to agree that she might be right on that point.

"Tell me more about Harbottle's friend, the one living in the Cotswolds who vouches for him."

"Oh! Yes, a very respected business man, well liked locally and living in a good style, no trouble there I'm sure—I've his name somewhere—ah, here it is—a Mr Harold Carter and his wife Muriel, they were perfectly sure that Harbottle had been there that night."

Harold—Harold? A bell rang in Annie's mind. This couldn't be Harry could it? Roughly speaking they were both in this, weren't they or were they? She asked the Inspector, "Could he be Harry? If so I've heard a lot about a Harry."

The Inspector again consulted his notes, "His wife apparently called him Harry, or so the sergeant who interviewed him says, but what of it, it's a common name?"

"I know and I grant you it could be just a coincidence, it's only one of those prickly feelings which happen and sometimes . . ." Annie paused. "Rose came in last night," she went on seeing that she had the Inspector's interest even if he was not convinced, "She's been working on our friend Harbottle, on the computer that is, after finding out so much about that hidden equipment. She wants to talk to you anyway, she thinks Mr H never was the philanthropist he claimed to be, it was only talk and people believed him. May I suggest you talk to Rose, get her to work on this Harold Carter and ask Janet Lucas, one of the nurses, for Harry's surname. Be suspicious if she says Smith."

As Matron came in the Inspector left, he felt unsure but it was a line of enquiry he couldn't ignore.

"I wish," said Clare, "that things would happen one at a time. We've three situations and none of them remotely connected." She didn't wait for any answer as she busied herself making tea for them both.

"Don't be too sure," said Annie firmly.

Ignoring this, Clare went on, "Firstly all this missing-and-now-found equipment and drugs, then Mrs Harbottle's death. Obviously someone got in and we don't know who . . ."

Annie interrupted, "It was the husband, and he knew how to get in."

"You can't be so sure of that."

"Oh! Yes, it's easy, a white coat, a stethoscope."

"And I understand a watertight alibi," Clare questioned with a pointed laugh.

"Tell them to take that with a pinch of salt," Annie recommended.

Clare handed her a cup of tea while considering this. "And the baby business?" she asked.

"The baby swapping?" Annie was thoughtful. "I believe—mind you it's only a guess—I believe she did that to take people off the track and on the night the goods were going to be moved. I hope there's a guard on that now."

"There is, Inspector David has a rota of keen-eyed young policemen, their very presence is upsetting the nurses."

Annie laughed but continued, "All connected, you see, she would have been murdered if she threatened to spill the beans."

"You can't know this can you?"

"Of course not but it fits neatly and eventually Inspector David will reach the same conclusions. Are there any biscuits, I'm sure I saw you with a tin?" she asked as she drank her tea.

There was a knock on the door, Inspector David put his head round it, and he seemed bewildered.

"Do you fancy a cup of tea?" Clare asked him.

"I'd love one," he said as he came in. To Annie he said, "Yes it was Smith but she saw Carter on some papers, she spent that night with him in a hotel, can it really be true?"

"See what Rose can do, she's a wizard at finding out things."

"I'll do that but I shall go up to the Cotswolds myself, I'm sure my wife will find somewhere nice to stay, she might even come with me."

D.I. David decided that a talk with Rose couldn't do any harm, he sat for a moment drinking his tea and contemplating a pleasant trip to a part of the country he loved. "Duty calls," he said cheerfully as he left. Much more cheerfully than when he came in, thought Annie.

Rose wasn't at all surprised when he spoke of Harold Carter. "Annie and I have come to the same conclusion on this and yes, I've already found out quite a bit about them both—that is Harbottle and Carter. We know that they are connected and even working together."

"Do we?"

"We know that Harry is a receiver of stolen goods, we've already broken this alibi, or you will when you work on it. Harbottle never was the philanthropist he claimed to be, it was only talk and people believed him. This stuff he said he had given to the hospital, clever that, a document to say it had been delivered, he then removes it and sells it to another hospital; a check with the big County Hospital would be a good idea. He steals it or tries to on the night of the baby swapping. Annie and I think the wife did that. Unfortunately for him, or them, the new Matron had arrived and everything was locked up, even the keys . . . wife threatens to tell, gets murdered . . ."

"You've lost me. If only it was true but it's too neat, it can't be right."

"Why not? Everything must fit if it's true. A bit of luck for me because Dudley knew Harry, have a chat with Dud, you'll learn a lot. So—over to you."

CHAPTER 9

"I'VE A GOOD MIND TO lock you in," Clare told Annie, "you're looking very flushed again and there's too much going on in here. You'd be better off at home only I do so enjoy having you here, the office is a hive of industry and in here it isn't quite so noisy. I can think in here and enjoy, with you, a quiet cup of tea. Have you had supper, I hope you aren't neglected because you're off the normal route?"

"I'm fine," Annie reassured her, "and yes, I've had supper. I feel a different kind of tiredness, I shall sleep well I know. If I look flushed it's because it's a bit warmer. I'm much better, I know it."

"I'll leave you then, see you in the morning."

The sun was shining when Annie woke, there had been talk of a Zimmer frame and didn't Clare say that she would be better off at home. Not long now she thought, and with both Sally and Bob there nothing could possibly go wrong and it is a bungalow. So she comforted herself. It was late, why had no-one been in? Where was breakfast or Clare to make tea? I've overslept, where is everyone? Had Clare locked her in?

Clare broke into her thoughts, she came in with a rush and full of distress, "You'll never guess, you'll not believe it, there's been another baby swapping incident, but this time there seems to be a missing one, we're searching for it now. This puts paid to your idea that it was Mrs Harbottle."

"Not at all," said Annie defensively, "It's obviously a copy-cat crime."

"Copy-cat crime you think, but who and why? I must say you're always full of theories. We're still looking for the missing one, the Mothers are all in a panic again and I can't say I blame them. I'm glad you haven't got it?

"Where was the duty nurse?" Annie asked.

"Apparently visiting the duty policeman in the outbuilding, she's in tears and resigning." Matron sighed, "I'll organize your breakfast, she shall bring it, and you can question her if you like."

Breakfast came; it was brought in by a tearful looking nurse who made sure that Annie was comfortable, "What's your name?" asked Annie.

"I'm Daphne Cook and yes, I'm the one who . . .,"

"It'll blow over," Annie reassured her. "Everyone makes mistakes, I shouldn't resign." Annie's tone was enough for Daphne to know that she had a sympathetic listener. "He was so cold, there's no heating down there."

"He'll be in trouble, too, if he left his post to seek a warm drink, he could have taken a thermos, or maybe he fancied a bit of company."

Daphne turned away to hide a smile, "That Inspector isn't here. There's going to be the woman sergeant in charge of the case, she may be more understanding."

"I'm sure she will be," said Annie thinking Tracy made a bad mistake and paid for it. Then a horrible thought struck her—too late to ask Daphne who had left, closing the door behind her.

Was it a boy or a girl baby who was missing? Annie remembered Rose's story of someone wanting a baby and who had gone to Romania to find one. Rose had even suggested that Dudley thought it a good idea, you could be sure of the sex you wanted. They had Victoria

Grace and now they wanted a boy, they couldn't possibly have been so stupid as to steal one from here, having had the idea from the previous incident. No, No, impossible, but Neil was no longer here to block such a scheme. Annie had to know, she rang her bell. It was Matron followed closely by Sergeant Williams who answered it.

"Was it a boy or a girl—the missing one?" she asked.

"A lovely little girl, dark and beautiful, why?" said Matron, "Why do you want to know?"

"Just a thought I had," she replied, relief flooding over her—it would have to have been a boy—a blond boy if she knew Dudley. Annie returned to her breakfast more cheerfully and without replying.

"So who is it this time?" asked Tracy with a half-mocking laugh. She grinned broadly, "Don't tell me you don't know?" she teased.

"Oh! Yes," Annie retorted, "better get on to it fast before she does a runner."

Tracy's grin vanished, "Are you serious?"

"Never more so!"

"You said it was a copy-cat crime. Who's doing the copying? Who is the culprit?"

"That so called Italian woman of course, ask to see her passport."

"A passport?" queried Tracy.

"A passport?" repeated Clare, "What's that to do with it."

"It should be an Italian one shouldn't it and she should have it with her," Annie explained.

"It's worth a try I suppose," said Tracy in a disbelieving voice, "if you say so." She left.

"It's your case, I'm not involved," Annie called after her.

Tracy arrived at Waverley Ward to see that Francesca Massarotti, the name at the end of her bed, was telling a nurse what to pack. "Are you leaving us Senora?" asked Tracy. She looked hard at Francesca and laughed.

"All that make-up doesn't suit you Fanny," she said, "because that's who you are isn't it?" And adding in her official voice, "Fanny Small I'm arresting you for . . ., she paused. To the nurse she said

"Please fetch the Matron and if possible two of the policemen who are helping in the baby search, this patient isn't leaving at the moment?

"You could do with a good wash," she said to Fanny. "I heard you were out, back at your old tricks. It's a good thing I spotted you."

"You've nothing against me," said Fanny. "Doing a bit of acting isn't a crime."

"Suspected baby snatching and wasting police time will do for a start." Tracy was triumphant.

"Or disturbing the peace," suggested the patient in the next bed and was applauded by the rest of the ward.

Annie's mind was on her Zimmer frame when Tracy, Rose, Dudley and Clare joined her. Dudley found more chairs and Clare put the kettle on.

"What made you suspect her?" asked Rose.

Annie thought for a bit, 'Bernard told me in a feverish dream' didn't sound very convincing but she felt she must give Bernard some credit. "Bernard and I spent many holidays in Italy, we even spoke a bit of Italian. We loved it there, beautiful countryside and fascinating walks. We also loved the Italian people, some perhaps a bit noisy by our standards but not so brash as our so-called Francesca. Some of her words weren't right, she'd learnt it up for the occasion, it was overdone, out of character, fishy as Dudley would tell us. I was suspicious of her from the beginning so it was fairly obvious. She got the idea from the previous baby business but if Tracy will tell us the whole . . ."

"I sure will," interrupted Tracy. "She is one of a gang of people traffickers. We've set the ball rolling and have heard already that the baby is safe and on her way back here. There'll be a very disappointed family, for I expect she was being sold and a goodish sum will already have been paid."

Annie was glad to hear Rose mutter, "disgraceful."

"She only got six months," Tracy continued. "I had heard she was out but never thought she'd be back on her old game. Mrs Butcher is probably right that the idea of coming in here and copying the baby swapping occurred to her as being a clever idea, never very original was our Fanny."

"She'll get another six months I suppose," said Dudley.

"She may get more this time and she may lead us to more of the gang, particularly those at the top we didn't get last time."

"This'll do you a bit of good," said Dudley. "You properly bungled it last time—remember?"

Tracy didn't want to remember, she looked at Annie daring her to say anything but Annie looked away remembering very well, for it had meant the loss of her swimming companion when Tracy was moved. Hopes of promotion had been squashed when Tracy had gone in to a scene from which she'd been told to keep away She was being used in an undercover plan and in disguise but couldn't resist being there in full uniform to triumph over the evil crowd she so much disliked and had had to work with.

'Into the valley of death,' thought Annie, remembering how Tracy, with buttons ablaze, shoes polished to brilliance, cap firmly forward, had marched in with the arresting officers.

"I'm sure I'll be forgiven now," declared Tracy, sitting up very straight and catching Annie's eye at last.

"Good for you," said Annie with a smile.

The rain came and helped to clear the remaining snow. Now that the roads were no longer a problem, traffic flowed freely and everything was returning to normal and, except for the presence of the police still, this included the hospital. Schools now reopened as did the college. The hospital staff all returned and more visitors came to see the patients, they brought outside news and many terrifying tales of their sufferings. "How lucky you were to be in a nice warm hospital," was the general theme.

Matron decided to make an appointment herself, the computer operator hadn't returned and she asked Rose if she would become a permanent member of the staff. This offer didn't include Dudley, she felt that in all probability he would be around anyway although she had never been quite sure of his obviously self-appointed part in the running of the hospital. Rose accepted the post on the understanding that Victoria Grace would come with her, an idea welcomed by all the nurses for Victoria Grace was a charmer.

Annie was making excellent progress and felt it was time she was home. Matron kept telling her not to hurry but Maggie's description of the supply teacher in the biology department was not reassuring. "I'll be back soon," Annie told Maggie.

Superintendent Neil LaCoste came to stay with Dudley and Rose for a weekend. This was not his patch or any of the events his 'case'. Inspector David was back, congratulating Tracy on her remarkable achievement not only in finding the arbitrator of the crime which possibly could lead to knowledge and possible arrest of some much wanted criminals. He himself was receiving congratulations for having solved or being on the brink of solving (the mystery) of the missing articles and drugs, not only that but linking it to the murder of the culprit's wife. He had been congratulated on having so neatly connected the events and he, too, was looking forward to promotion.

"I recognize the hand behind this," Neil said to Dudley.

"Yes," replied Dudley, "I thought you might, though one has to admit that it was Sergeant Williams who recognized this Fanny Small woman."

"Ah, just the thinking part then. She was right, too, on the murder in her old room for both Inspector David and I thought that Annie was the target."

Matron was growing suspicious of the continual presence of the Superintendent, "Is there anything in it?" she asked Rose.

"Not my business," answered Rose discouragingly.

Annie was determined to get moving and to go home, she suspected Clare of trying to keep her there for friendship's sake for there was no doubt of their getting on so well together, but Rose was here now, and between them they were creating a solid nucleus of good administration. They would present a united front when the threatened new administrator was appointed.

Annie was practicing on her Zimmer frame in the corridors when she met a lost-looking visitor.

"Can I help you?" she asked.

"I doubt it," he replied looking doubtfully at her means of mobility.

"Try me, you don't know unless you do," she suggested in her best teaching manner.

"I'm looking for Matron," he said uneasily.

What's the matter with the man Annie wondered, she reassured him cheerfully. "She's in my room, follow me."

Matron was there, she looked enquiringly at Annie.

"This gentleman is looking for you," Annie told her.

"I'm a private detective," he said.

"Oh! Good, meet another one," Matron indicated Annie.

"She's joking," protested Annie. "I'm a teacher or I am when I haven't broken my leg."

"What I meant was—you can talk freely in front of her, she's very discreet. May I know your name?"

The visitor—this private detective—sighed, "I'll tell you," he said, "if you promise not to comment on it."

They looked at him with frowning bewildered looks. "We won't say a word," said Clare.

"It's Watson."

"What of that, it's a common enough name?"

"I'm known as Johnny, my first name is John you see, I'm not a doctor, can't think what my parents were thinking of but I'm not a doctor, so you see . . ."

"I do see," Annie acknowledged, "but he was only a fictional narrator, after all."

Clare smiled, "How can we help you?" she asked.

"I'm working for a Mrs Carter, unpleasant case, divorce in the offing, that's all I seem to get."

"Someone has to do it," said Rose as she came into the room, she had been standing in the doorway.

"I was a businessman until I retired," he confessed. "Thought I'd take it up as a hobby, my name gave me the idea."

"What is it you want here?" enquired Clare again. "Can we be of any help?"

"I've been asked by a Mrs Harold Carter to look into—well not exactly looking into—more snooping . . ."

"Not a very nice word," put in Annie

"The only sort of work I seem to get, this isn't a very pleasant case, its divorce you see," John Watson sighed. "She wants me to try and get in touch with a nurse she thinks works here. She, Mrs Carter, gave a friend of her husband an alibi, she now says he wasn't there and neither was the husband, he'd persuaded her, she now withdraws that statement and is trying to cover herself by saying she mistook the night. The husband needs one himself now, or so the Inspector on the case has discovered. As I said it's a nasty business for the friend is suspected of murder. Yes murder!" he brightened considerably. "I've not had a murder case before, or been on the borders of one."

Annie and Clare looked at each other, "Is that Inspector David?" asked Clare.

John Watson seemed surprised. "That's him," he replied. "He thinks that the husband—this Mr Carter—was at a hotel with a nurse from here. Mrs Carter has been thinking of divorce for some time as she doesn't like some of her husband's activities. She expects to do reasonably well out of it, she's paying me handsomely as there's plenty of attractive and desirable property, some in London, which when sold, which it will have to be, will see that she is—well—well provided for." He paused, "So if this girl is willing to give evidence Mrs Carter would . . ."

"Bribe her?" interrupted Clare.

"Certainly not," Mr Watson was very shocked. "I was about to say offer her assistance—generous assistance—in any expenses she might incur."

"Naturally," returned Clare.

Annie and Clare again exchanged glances. "I will see if Nurse Lucas is about and willing to see you." Clare left.

John Watson's eyes followed her, to Annie he said, "What a very fine woman, is she—er—is she married?"

Annie thought I don't think much of him as a detective, Sherlock would definitely have known.

Clare returned. "If you would care to come into my office, Nurse Lucas will join you there, that is when she is off duty." She turned to Annie, "A visitor for you," she announced.

Annie was glad to see that it was Neil.

"You're on your feet at last," he said cheerfully.

"Not exactly," she said, "but it's a step forward."

"There's a wheelchair just down the corridor, I'll fetch it and we'll go down to the café. I just heard two visitors talking and say that coffee was quite something, by that I took it they meant . . ."

Annie interrupted him, "I'd love a good coffee, I'm getting sick of tea, Oh No!" she suddenly exclaimed.

"What is it?" he asked.

"Up until this week Sally has been running the café. 'Good Coffee' you said. What's the betting it's that wonderful Kenya coffee we brought back with us."

Neil laughed, "Don't worry, I brought some back too. I'll get that wheelchair."

He returned with the wheelchair, he picked her up and placed her in it before she could protest. She tried to do so but found to her dismay that her feeling of enjoyment far outweighed her feelings of protestation. She was appalled at herself but let herself be taken to the hospital coffee shop.

The coffee was good, "Some left by the girl who ran this place when I couldn't get in," was the explanation given by the present volunteer.

"I thought as much," said Annie as she drank the excellent brew.

"The man you saw was a private detective," she told Neil. "I hope that Inspector David won't mind him, he didn't strike me as being over brilliant. He's also an admirer of the Matron, Rose overheard some of this so I expect she will find out more about him. He asked if Clare was married, Rose will put her own interpretation on that."

Neil laughed, "Tell me more," he said encouragingly.

"He told us he was retired and because his name was John Watson decided to become a private detective, I've no doubt he was bored but it didn't seem a logical or obvious sequel or reason."

"What did he retire from?"

Rose entered at that moment, rumours of good coffee having reached her. "Found out the name of his firm," she said. "It's Cruickshank, Watson & Fielding in Manchester."

"I've heard of them," said Neil. "They recently retired one of the founder members because there were many younger members of the family waiting to join the firm. He had a good bonus I remember, as well as his pension."

"How much is a good bonus?" asked Annie.

"About two million I think it was, may have been more."

Annie was speechless.

"I'm glad I asked him if he was musical," said Rose. "He replied that he used to play the oboe so I suggested he got practicing."

Annie found her voice, "Maybe the firm wanted to get rid of him," she suggested.

"He could be very useful here," said Rose thoughtfully.

They were all thoughtful when Sally joined them.

"Hi," she greeted them cheerily, "so you've made it as far as here. Is there any of that decent coffee left?" she sniffed loudly, "Ah! good, I can smell it."

"Is there any of it left at home?" asked Annie, but without hope.

"Nope, but who cares, we've plenty of friends out there now and who knows—Bob and I might be going back there sometime, a honeymoon perhaps."

"Oh! Is there a wedding in the offing?" asked Annie, thinking—I suppose they'd let me know.

"Have you heard from Joel?" Sally seemed to be changing the subject but Annie was suspicious.

"Is this a continuation of the wedding subject?" she enquired.

"Possibly, she's pregnant you know, and I think they'd like to have it all legal."

It's time I was home thought Annie, things have been going on without me, I need to be back in the running. She was lost for the moment thinking of the joys of grandmahood and buying delightful little garments.

"I don't know what to do," Sally was saying to her Mother as Neil fetched coffee for them all. "Bob's uncle has offered us his flat, he's been offered a position in a London Hospital, he's accepted it as he can be with his family again. But what about you, shall you be okay?"

"I'm going to stay with Dudley and Rose for a while, Maggie offered but with four kids, she doesn't need an invalid as well."

"Are you likely to be around?" Sally asked Neil.

"Almost certainly," he replied with a satisfied smile.

"Want to hear my other news?" Sally asked Annie.

"Fire away," answered Annie with her mind on Neil's decisive words, there was a firm determined look on his face too, which she couldn't ignore.

Sally continued, totally unaware of any under-currents. "It's good news, Matron has offered me a job, a sort of dogs-body, general slave, helping her and Rose. I've accepted, it'll do me fine until September when I start at Uni. I'd even do a bit of cleaning if necessary. Bob thinks it's great and I'd be around here for you because you're going to be in lots more pain before you're finished."

"Oh! Thank you very much," responded Annie. "If you did want my advice about the flat then yes, accept that too. I assure you I'm going to be just fine."

Mrs David enjoyed her occasional voluntary work at the hospital especially during the weather crisis when she felt herself really wanted. Everything was back to normal now.

"How are things up at the hospital?" she asked her husband, "anything happening?"

"Nothing much," the Inspector replied, "everything's going according to plan. Funny thing though, a private detective has arrived, paid by a wife sick of her husband's activities. He's waving money around and conducting his own interviews. He's not doing the sort of thing I could do but he's been willing to share his results and boy, has he got results. His name is Watson, he's retired but I've no idea what from."

"How is Mrs Butcher, is she still there?"

"Won't be long now I'm sure. Very sensible woman—Mrs Butcher," he paused but seeing he had his wife's whole attention he continued. "We've got the Harbottle man on a charge of murder, we're sure now that he did it, and that Harry Carter for aiding and abetting, both for stealing and wasting police time. You remember

Sergeant Williams, I'm sure, well she recognized the woman who did the baby stealing, a Fanny Small who already had done a term for people trafficking, she'd only just come out. The baby's safe I'm sure you'd want to know," the Inspector paused.

"And you call that 'nothing much'," his wife protested, "I hope you get promotion."

His wife was a bit of a gossip so that there was plenty he did not tell her, it was probably only idle chat that this John Watson was a millionaire and the rumour said he was an admirer of the Matron. He had seen her totting up a lot of figures but that could mean anything. He had been several times to see Mrs Butcher but she was not one to gossip, it was true that she saw things in a different way and often came up with the right answer. Sheer luck of course, maybe as a teacher she was able to see through difficulties. She had been very quiet and thoughtful, probably in pain again. He told himself that it would be a good thing if his wife did return, then she could sort out all the rumours for herself. He wondered what she would make of Superintendent LaCoste who was going about so starry-eyed that there was no getting any sense out of him at all.